STRANDED WITH ELLA

A STEAMY SMALL TOWN ROMANCE

SHELLEY MUNRO

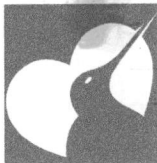

MUNRO PRESS

Stranded with Ella

Copyright © 2024 by Shelley Munro

Print ISBN: 978-1-99-106348-9
Digital ISBN: 978-0-473-47455-3

Editor: Evil Eye Editing

Cover: Kim Killion, The Killion Group, Inc.

Munro Press, New Zealand.

First Munro Press electronic publication March 2019

First Munro Press print publication March 2024

DEDICATION

For Paul, my partner in crime and fellow adventurer.

INTRODUCTION

A ghost propels them together. Danger will try to rip them apart...

Ella Liddington-Walsh is turning quietly—make that noisily—insane, and it is all soldier Dillon Williams's fault because the ghost harassing Ella belongs to HIM. Sleep-deprived and desperate, she drives to his country property to confront the man. One way or another, she will pass on her problem and *finally* sleep through the entire night. Not that her task will be easy since Dillon strikes her as a no-nonsense military man. A believer in ghosts—not so much.

Widower Dillon judges Ella's pink hair, her weird stories of haunting and decides she's crazy. He sends her packing, but a landslide brings the sassy lady returning like a boomerang. Unable to deny her shelter during the stormy night, he discovers an unwilling fascination and attraction

1

for the curvy Ella, along with common ground and whoa! Steamy hijinks in his big bed.

After his wife's murder, Dillon isn't looking for romance, but a chance discovery brings the past and the present on a collision. Dillon realizes he likes Ella more than he should, and if he doesn't stay alert, he'll lose her in the same way he lost his wife.

Contains a determined, vintage-wearing heroine and a grumpy soldier who wears guilt like a second skin. On paper, they shouldn't work but there's no accounting for the power of attraction and a landslide blocking the road.

1

MEETING THE SOLDIER, EKETAHUNA, NEW ZEALAND

ELLA LIDDINGTON-WALSH YAWNED—A MOUTH wide, jaw-busting attempt to pump oxygen into her sleep-deprived body. Visions of her cozy bed floated through her mind as she pulled from the employee parking lot at Pukaha Mt. Bruce National Wildlife Center. Instead of turning left toward her cottage, she opened the window and drove right. The blast of frigid winter air did the trick, and by the time she indicated another right turn, her foggy fatigue had lifted a fraction.

Instead, nerves danced a spirited tango in the pit of her stomach. Dillon Williams would call her crazy. She'd glimpsed the big, bearded soldier from a distance last week. One of her girlfriends had whispered this was the oldest Williams son, and he was home on leave. A single look had told her this military man's bullshit meter would ping the instant she poured out her unlikely tale.

A tremor spread from her arms to her fingertips, and in self-defense, she tightened her grip on the wheel.

Heck, *she'd* pooh-pooh her story.

The tarmac gave way to gravel as the narrow country road twisted and turned up a valley and deeper into the hills surrounding the Eketahuna region. Pastureland grew steadily rougher and soon native bush crammed the spaces and towered overhead, darkening the road as it scaled yet another hill. Ella flicked on her headlights.

"How much farther is this house?" she muttered as her compact car shuddered up the steep grade.

When she'd convinced herself she'd missed the driveway, she spotted a white farmhouse with a curl of smoke drifting from the chimney. The building nestled against trees while half a dozen alpaca grazed in a paddock to the left of the house. One of the smaller animals jumped and leaped, enjoying the last of the day's sparse sunshine.

A black utility vehicle—the type of monster transport owned by most of the farming families in the district—sat on the rutted driveway.

This must be it. Dillon's mother had given her directions when Ella had attempted to phone Dillon. Evidently, cell phone coverage was spotty, which was why Ella hadn't managed to connect earlier.

Marlene Williams had asked lots of nosy questions and confided Dillon worried her and her husband, especially since his wife's murder. An in-person visit with someone his own age would do her son good. And how had they

4

met?

Ella had mumbled her way through a stupid excuse about a search of his land for kiwis. Total rubbish of course, and she suspected Mrs. William saw right through her. She'd assumed Ella wanted her son for different reasons and had encouraged the interaction. Renewed embarrassment fired Ella's cheeks with heat as she replayed that mortifying phone call.

Marlene Williams had practically urged Ella to seduce her son.

That was unlikely, given her experience and track record with men. Best to stick to friends only and leave the romance to others. Her circle of friends, along with her pursuits of handicrafts and her job at the wildlife center, which she adored, all kept her busy.

However, if she wanted an uninterrupted night's sleep, she had to speak with the taciturn Dillon Williams.

With a sigh, Ella eyed the gate blocking the driveway and the potholes beyond. Several of them appeared large enough to swallow her car. Perhaps she should park here and walk the rest of the way. Decision made, she pulled up in front of the gate and switched off the ignition. She hesitated. No, dithered.

This situation had disaster written all over it.

"Stop procrastinating, Ella. You will never have peace if you don't do this." After a deep inhalation, she opened the door and climbed out. Her favorite boots sank into three inches of mud, and she groaned.

Great. Just great.

Determined to create a positive impression, she'd

changed at work into one of her favorite vintage dresses and a houndstooth swing coat. She should've stuck with her comfy uniform of polo shirt, jeans, and gumboots.

Ella yanked her leather boots from the mud. Sanity prevailed, and she stomped through yet more mud to her trunk. Creating a favorable impression wasn't worth ruining her expensive boots. She did an ungainly one-legged stork hop as she exchanged muddy leather boots for practical gumboots.

Every instinct told her to forget this mission and return to her cottage. Who needed sleep anyway?

A sudden blast of frigid air struck her in the face. Her skin turned to goose flesh, the hair at her nape prickling with preternatural unease.

"Okay. *Okay*. I'm going." Ella stomped to the gate and let herself through. She weaved her way past potholes filled with water and patches of mud and congratulated herself on not attempting to drive to the house.

A low growl froze her on the spot. Her gaze jumped from the mud puddle at her feet to the big, shaggy gray dog regarding her like its next dinner.

"Good doggie." Ella's voice trembled. She was so not a dog person. Give her a purring cat, a sexy romance on her e-reader, a glass of wine and call her happy. "G-good d-doggie."

"What the hell are you doing?" a harsh voice demanded.

Ella's tense muscles melted in relief. Soldier to the rescue. "I-I... Dillon Williams?" She recognized him, of course, but one didn't plunge willy-nilly into a conversation of this sort.

"I repeat, what are you doing here?" In the rapidly dimming light, he was huge. Despite the cold, he wore a gray T-shirt covered by a red-and-black check flannel shirt. No coat for the tough soldier. A bushy black beard hid his features, but his bright blue eyes fired salvos of distrust.

"I need to talk to you, Dillon." There, that had sounded positive and assertive.

"If you want to fuck a soldier, you've come to the wrong one. I'm not interested. Go, before I let Rufus say hello."

"I-I—what? Why would you presume that?" Ella's voice rose to chipmunk heights in her disbelief.

"You're not the first," he snapped.

"For your information, I prefer my men well-groomed and at least half-tame. You are neither. Are you going to invite me in or not? Look, I don't want to be here, but I need sleep. So bad. I had to drive here with the window open to stay awake. I…" Aware she was babbling, Ella trailed off.

To cap things off, it started to rain. Not delicate drops but hard, driving bullets of water.

Dillon cursed.

Ella sucked in a breath and tried again. "Please. Let me talk, then I'll leave. You might have a sexy body, but I have no designs on it. Truly, you're not my type."

Dillon snorted and clicked his fingers at the dog. "I can spare you five minutes before I feed the alpacas and get them into the shelter for the night."

"Thank you," Ella said, but Dillon had turned his back and was striding away, stepping over the puddles with ease.

The dog growled, baring sharp white teeth, before

following his master.

Ella tackled the rest of the driveway, thankful for her gumboots. Her gaze jumped to the man's jeans-clad backside. Fuck a soldier, indeed. She'd rather kick his sexy, muscular arse. Big oaf!

Breathless with the rapid ascent of the last bit of the sloped driveway, Ella was panting when she reached the impatient soldier. "I don't have long legs."

"Your legs look fine," he said.

With any other man, she'd have expected a wink or at least a smile. Dillon Williams did neither, which left her floundering.

"We'll talk in here," he said, gesturing toward the carport.

"Fine." She got it. She didn't want to be here any more than he wanted her on his property.

Ella stepped out of the rain. The hard splatters rattled against the iron roof. Her gaze zapped to Dillon.

The man folded his arms over his wide chest. The gray dog sat at his feet, the canine's amber eyes alert and watching her every move.

Such a warm welcome.

"Well," Dillon demanded in a not-so-silent prod for her to get talking.

"I-I don't k-know where to start."

"The beginning."

"Thank you, Mr. Obvious."

He inclined his head, his big hand rubbing behind the dog's ears.

Thoughts of those hands stroking her body popped into

her mind, and she jerked away her gaze. A croak wriggled its way up her tight throat. She coughed and tried again.

"I've been having dreams."

Dillon snorted.

"Will you give me a chance? This is difficult enough without your smartarse commentary."

"Yes, ma'am."

"There is a woman haunting me," Ella blurted. "Every night. I'm not getting any sleep. And she says she won't leave me alone until I give you a message. That's why I'm here."

"A ghost?" His dark brows rose above those bright eyes of his. Suspicion radiated off him in waves.

Ella swallowed, her gaze settling on her muddy boots. She'd guessed at his disbelief. Who in their right mind believed in ghosts? "She said I should tell you not to blame yourself, that you have to move on with the future."

"The ghost said this?"

"Yes, she said it's not your fault. Okay, I've delivered the message, and I'm going now."

Ella stepped from the carport's shelter. Rain pelted her hot cheeks, and she welcomed the chilly blast.

Strong fingers banded around her biceps, yanking her to a halt.

"Lady, you're a piece of work. What is your game?"

"No game," Ella took a giant step back, pulling from the contact. "I'm leaving, and you'll never need to deal with me again. Promise." Ella turned her back, holding her breath as she made her escape. This time, he let her depart, and she trekked to the gate and her vehicle in double-time.

She jumped in her car and grabbed a packet of tissues from her handbag. She wiped her wet face, dragged on the seatbelt and started her car for the journey home. Once there, she'd shower, have a glass of wine, and forget the rude soldier and this entire crazy situation.

It was much darker now, the wet conditions making driving difficult. Ella drove at a snail's pace, confident she was the only idiot on the road in this weather.

"I hope you're satisfied." Ella had no idea whether the woman haunting her was listening. "He thought I was a fruit-loop. I knew it. Men like him only understand the tangible things right in front of their faces."

Lightning flashed, illuminating the road for an instant. Thunder rattled her little car and nudged her anxiety a notch higher. Storms always pushed vulnerabilities to the surface. They brought back memories of her parents who'd died in an accident during a winter storm. Ella slowed a fraction more, steering to the middle of the road. After a week of inclement weather, today had been sunny. A promise of spring. Now, Mother Nature was thumbing her nose at everyone again.

Ella crossed a narrow one-lane bridge, the stream beneath a raging torrent. She rounded a corner.

"Danger!"

An icy chill crawled across Ella's limbs. Fear lurched her stomach, tightened her chest, and she slammed on the brakes. A loud roar penetrated the car. A second later, the headlights flickered out and darkness filled Ella's vision. Silence fell, and her heart thundered in her ears. After a long moment, she attempted to open the driver's door. It refused to budge.

Ella removed her seatbelt and scrambled over the console separating her from the passenger seat. The door on this side opened without a hiccup. She tumbled out, her breath catching once she realized what had happened.

A landslide.

Horror flooded her as rain flattened her hair and water dripped down her face. If she hadn't stopped when she had, she'd be buried beneath that huge pile of dirt and trees. A flash of lightning showed her the scale of the problem. The entire hill had come away and now obstructed the road. She doubted she'd free her car, given the mountain of earth and flora blocking the way. No way to make it to her cottage tonight, which left one alternative.

She'd have to plead with Mr. Grumpy to give her shelter.

Ella grabbed her handbag. While her phone mightn't work in this maze of hills, at least it held a full charge, so she could use the torch app.

She wasn't sure how far she'd driven—two or three kilometers from Dillon Williams's property. A soft groan squeezed past her trembling lips. That meant she had a decent walk in front of her. With her handbag hitched over one shoulder, she sloshed through puddles and jumped each time lightning lit the night sky and thunder echoed through the hills. Water seeped into her dress and slid under the collar of her coat. Cold sank into her bones. Ella forced herself onward and tried not to dwell on bogeymen who lived in the dark.

After a hot shower, Dillon studied the contents of his fridge with disinterest. Finally, he selected a container of beef stew. With his alpacas fed and under shelter, he had nothing pressing to do for the rest of the evening. Restlessness kept him from planting himself in front of the telly, a sense of something about to happen bringing uneasiness. Those spidey senses at work.

That woman...

She refused to leave his mind. Not his sort. Too weird with her talk of ghosts and the bright pink streaks in her light brown hair. Nice figure, but the type of woman that caused too much trouble for him to bother.

A ghost.

He shook his head. How the hell did she expect him to buy that bullshit story?

No doubt, the local gossip featuring him had reached her, and she'd hit upon an original way of approach. Newsflash—her plan had bombed, just as the other local women had failed to attract his interest. He pulled a pot from a cupboard and transferred the stew. Perhaps he'd strip the old paper off the walls in here. He and Hana had planned to redecorate one room at a time. At least, he'd keep busy.

Hell. Life was so much simpler when he was with his team.

But Hana's death, the snafu that had been his last mission... He'd needed time out to get his head straight. He knew this instinctively without letting the medical experts poke at his brain. So he'd applied for leave, coming home to sort himself out and recharge. A return to the house where his wife had been murdered. His mother had protested, wanting him to stay at the family home. He'd refused the offer.

This was his land, and he needed something to do, so it made sense to stay here and work. Sure, he missed the easy friendship he'd experienced with Hana, an interpreter he'd met while in Afghanistan, but he hadn't loved her. Theirs had been a marriage of convenience although they'd done an excellent job of pretending otherwise for family and officials. After dissidents had shot the rest of Hana's family, Dillon had wanted her safe in New Zealand, so they'd married.

For Hana to die in a senseless home invasion...

Dillon forced away the lump in his throat and placed the pot on the cooker to heat. Guilt filled him because she'd died in such a tragic manner, and he hadn't been here to protect her.

Rufus growled deep in his throat, diverting Dillon from his remorse. He dragged the stew off the heat and padded after the dog who waited at the front door. Dillon paused, then retreated to his bedroom to grab a handgun.

Someone thumped on the door. Rufus ceased his growling and barked instead. Dillon checked the safety and shoved the handgun at the back of his jeans. Although he doubted the thieves who'd murdered Hana six months ago and ransacked their house had returned, tension slid through his shoulders. Rufus barked again as he opened the door. The shaggy mutt charged through and knocked over his visitor before Dillon could order the dog to sit.

A feminine shriek cut through Rufus's barking.

"Rufus, heel!"

The mutt trotted to his side, sending him a chiding look as if Dillon had spoiled his fun.

Dillon stepped forward to aid his visitor. "You! What are you doing back here?"

Her hair plastered to her head and her dress and coat clung to her curves. Mud splattered her legs and the hem of her coat. Her cheeks were so pale, he noticed she had freckles on her nose. Her teeth chattered.

"L-landslide." She sniffed and her expression scrunched as if she might cry. "It buried most of my car."

"How far from the main road?"

"Um, two or three kilometers. My feet are killing me."

"Hell."

"I'm s-sorry. I h-had no place else to go."

As if he'd send her away in this weather. He might prefer his own company, but he wasn't a monster. "Come inside. You can have a hot shower while I find you dry clothes."

She removed her gumboots and stepped past him. Water dripped off her black-and-white coat. It trickled off her hair and ran down her cheek. Dillon bit back an inappropriate smile. He had a younger sister and experience told him now was not the time to display his amusement.

"This way." He strode along the passage leading to the bathroom. The woman thumped and blundered behind him, so he lengthened his stride and switched on the bathroom light. "What's your name?"

"Ella Liddington-Walsh."

"That's a mouthful."

Ella rolled her eyes at him. "My mother didn't want to lose her identity, and after a long discussion, my parents decided to each take the other's name and make it a true marriage."

"You been in Eketahuna long? We haven't met before."

"My family come from...came from Masterton."

Dillon spotted the flare of pain in her brown eyes when she mentioned her family and didn't prod. Instead, he opened a cupboard and pulled out towels. "I'll give you two towels in case you want to wash and dry your hair. Summer always used two."

"Summer?"

"My younger sister. She lives in Auckland. Check the cupboard for girly soap and shampoo." Dillon stopped talking. Her big brown eyes reminded him of a solemn owl. He was out of practice with females. Once he and Hana had married, he'd stopped tomcatting around, and after her death, it hadn't felt right to start again. Out of respect. He cleared his throat. "I'll leave clothes for you outside the door. Want something to eat?"

"No, thank you. I just want to get warm and sleep."

Crap. He only had one bed. Never mind. He'd worry later. "The bedroom is the one on the right at the end of the passage."

"Thanks. I'm sorry to be a nuisance."

Dillon confined himself to a nod. He'd cleared out Hana's clothes to give to the local hospice. They'd be too small for Ella. She'd have to make do with his sweatpants. In his bedroom, he sorted out a pair of boxer shorts and came across flannel pajamas his Grandma had given him for Christmas a few years ago. He added track-pants and a T-shirt to the pile for good measure, then escaped to the kitchen.

Ella's presence breathed weird energy into the atmosphere, and he disliked the disturbance. Not that he'd send her out into the night. His mother would've boxed his ears for even considering the offense.

Dillon stared at the stew and his unexpected guest jumped to mind again. Hot water bottle. The idea popped to mind along with a vague memory of a crocheted cover sitting in the back of the linen cupboard. He went to search, and it was right where his mind told him. Weird. With a shake of his head, he strode back to the kitchen to boil the jug.

A cup of tea. Maybe the drink would warm her.

Dillon froze. Now that thought hadn't come from the depths of his memory or had it? His mother and grandma were tea aficionados. The idea wasn't such a stretch, and he'd absorbed the niceties during his upbringing. While the jug was boiling, he searched through the pantry and came across a box of chamomile teabags. His gaze snagged on a travel mug.

Five minutes later, he placed the hot water bottle into the bed and set the travel mug on the bedside drawers.

The pile of clothes no longer sat at the bathroom door. Dillon paused en route for the kitchen. "I made you a cup of chamomile tea. It's sitting in the bedroom."

"Thank you."

Dillon continued to the kitchen. His belly rumbled and, with surprise, he realized he was hungry. Although he'd kept busy with outside chores and worked to maintain his fitness, he'd dropped weight. For the second time, he switched on the cooker and heated the stew. At the last minute, he grabbed a bag of snap-frozen vegetables from the freezer and microwaved a portion.

He sat at the kitchen table to eat. The table was new since his last visit, the wooden top lovingly varnished by Hana. Touches of his wife filled the farmhouse, bringing back treasured memories along with more guilt. The police hadn't caught the culprits and an exhaustive investigation had turned up nothing. His contact at the police station had informed him there'd been a home invasion at a property much closer to the township of Masterton. The one here had occurred three weeks later and none since. His mother had worried about Hana living here alone while Dillon was overseas. Hana had told everyone she loved the peace of the countryside and the green of the pastures and bush. She'd taken to bird watching and had delighted in the number of native birds she'd spotted around their home.

Her emails to him had been full of the new things she was trying, some with hilarious results, and the friends she'd made in the district. Hana had been so content here, the last words spoken between them ones of delight and appreciation. Dillon hadn't wanted her thanks. She and her family had done so much for his team, and he'd wanted to give her a slice of happiness in return.

Now she was dead

He swallowed hard to shift the obstruction blocking his throat and forked up more stew. He wished he could wind back time and change things, but Hana had fallen in love with his piece of land. It had been her idea to purchase alpacas so she could spin the fleece and transform it into garments. She'd fought for her independence, and he'd given in to her wish to live on his property. He'd decided it was safe since his parents had maintained regular contact with her.

Hana should've been secure here in New Zealand rather than the victim of a cowardly attack.

Dillon forced himself to eat the last of his meal and stood to do the few dishes. Once that was done, he checked on Ella.

The bedroom light still shone bright, but she was fast asleep. Now able to observe her without looking like a perv, he noted the violet shadows beneath her eyes. Dillon jiggled the travel mug and discovered it was empty, so he took it and retreated, turning off the light as he left.

Outside, the rain continued, although the thunder no longer echoed through the hills. Not ready to face sharing a bed with Ella, he spent an hour stripping wallpaper in the kitchen. And once he tired of this, he'd have a quiet beer, watch telly and send messages to his younger brother Josh and reply to Summer's email. If he sent the emails, his siblings would send favorable reports to his mother, which meant she'd ease up on the daily visits and twice-daily phone calls.

Dillon frowned. Tomorrow, he'd check out the landslide. Hopefully, Ella had exaggerated, and it wasn't as bad as she'd described. His frown deepened to a flat-out scowl. Had she lied to him?

He'd received three visits in the last two weeks from single ladies from the Eketahuna area plus two more indecent proposals from married women. Was Ella a liar?

He shook his head, recalling the shock on her pale face, the bruises beneath her eyes. If she'd had ulterior motives, she wouldn't have gone to bed as she had. She would've flirted with him, given him a glimpse of skin while covering her mouth with a shocked *oops*. Yeah, he'd been a recipient of all of those scenarios, and so far Ella Liddington-Walsh wasn't playing to the script.

Four hours later, Dillon padded into his bedroom and slipped between the sheets of his king-size bed. Ella didn't move or notice his arrival, and Dillon relaxed.

Recently, he hadn't slept well himself. Hopefully, his restlessness or, worse, one of his nightmares, didn't startle Ella awake.

2

BODY LANGUAGE

ELLA CAME AWAKE GRADUALLY, warm and snug in her bed. For the first time in ages, the ghost hadn't woken her with loud thumps and rattling pipes or chilly breezes, allowing her a refreshing night of rest. She stretched, stilling when she realized someone shared the bed with her. Her pulse raced a tad faster as she rifled through her mind, trying to recall the how and why. Not a memory surfaced. She came up empty. Not surprising, given she never functioned well on awakening. Her morning required a cup of tea to kick her brain into gear.

Ella fumbled for her bedside lamp, her hand waving at air. Then she remembered. She wasn't at home. This wasn't her bed.

So who the devil—?

"Stop fidgeting. It's still early," a masculine voice rumbled through the darkness.

"You! Why are you in my bed?" Ella attempted to scramble farther away and almost fell out of bed. "Ahh!"

"It's mine. You're in *my* bed," he corrected as his arm came around her waist and he hauled her back to her original position.

"The same one as me, you big oaf. Why are we in bed together?"

"Because it's the only one I have and I didn't want to freeze my arse off trying to sleep on the couch."

"I would've taken the couch."

He paused. "That makes no sense. You were asleep. I hated to wake you."

Ella swallowed, every muscle filled with tension. "That isn't your knee pushing into my backside."

He chuckled, the sound rusty as if he either didn't laugh much or hadn't for a long time. "I'm a male, honey. I can't help it."

"That's what all the men say," she muttered.

"Oh? Sleep with lots of men, do you?"

"That is not what I said. Can't you shift over, so I can get out of bed?"

"Why?"

"You're making me nervous."

Dillon shifted a fraction and removed his arm from around her waist. Unaccountably, she missed the contact straightaway.

"Apart from shifting in my sleep, I've done nothing to indicate I intend to rape you. My mother raised me better than that. I converse with my lovers before we have sex."

A scoffing sound escaped Ella. "You've never had a

one-night fling? Surely not. I've got eyes."

That arm slipped around her waist again, this time turning her body until they faced each other. Dark screened her view, but his citrus scent and manly musk filled her rapid breaths.

"What do your eyes tell you?" Humor filled his question. "Please answer. This week I've had a procession of uninvited female visitors."

"Is that why you were so rude to me?" Ella relaxed, eased by his amusement.

"Partly."

"My eyes tell me you're a handsome man and take after your father. In case you're wondering—I've met him at couple of times at local functions. You're big and fit and if we lived in the caveman days, I, along with every other cavewoman would queue to win you because of your muscular arse."

"I...what?"

Ella held back a giggle.

"What has my arse got to do with anything?" His tone held a touch of uneasiness.

She withheld a grin at his discomfort. "A muscular and tight masculine arse tells a woman this man has good forward propulsion, which is required to transfer sperm."

"Is that true?"

"I have a book on body language. We read it for book club last month."

"I'm unsure if I should be terrified or not. You mean to say the women in your local book club have read this book and checked out the available men?"

"Your mother goes to the book club."

Dillon said nothing for long seconds. "Change the subject. I do not want to picture my mother, backsides and sperm transfer in the same sentence ever again."

"Body language tells you a lot about a person."

"Obviously," he said. "You sound chirpy. Every time I woke during the night, you were snoring."

"I do not snore."

"You have no way of disproving me." He sounded distinctly smug.

"It's stopped raining." She pictured her car and the possible damage. "How long will it take to clear the road?"

"Months, if I know the local council."

"Months." Her horror echoed and bounced back to strike her brain for a second time. "You're joking."

"There are three properties on this road. The council will have other more important damage to repair."

"But how will I get home? I have work today. I can't stay here. My boss will worry because I'm reliable. Responsible."

Dillon said nothing for a while. "We'll get out a phone call or an email to tell people you're okay."

"My phone doesn't work here. I tried after...after I crawled out of my car and was in a safer place."

"I have a satellite phone for emergencies. It was for Hana."

Since she had been alone at the farm. Ella interpreted the subtext and understood without further explanations. Hana's murder had hit the national news and had occurred shortly before she'd moved to Eketahuna, and she'd picked up local gossip since. It was difficult not to tap into the local news and scandal. Her Masterton girlfriends had expressed horror at her decision to move closer to her job, but Ella hadn't regretted her decision. Her social life was busy these days, which reminded her.

"I have a date tonight and standing him up is mean. Wait—is it possible to walk home?"

"It's possible, but the forecast is for more rain."

"Oh." The thought of repeating her journey put a dampener on that plan. "I hate to inconvenience you."

"My bed was warm when I got into it last night. That's a plus."

Ella bit her lip. The sleep had recharged her, but she didn't want to share his bed for another night.

Somewhere outside, a dog barked.

Dillon groaned. "Rufus is my alarm clock. It must be seven. I can't believe I've slept this late."

"Haven't you been sleeping well either?"

"Bad dreams."

Succinct and to the point. Ella assumed he'd carry emotional luggage since he was on active duty. Local gossip said he was NZSAS, part of New Zealand's elite fighting soldiers. Only the best military men made it into the New Zealand Special Air Service. She understood the younger Williams brother was also SAS.

Dillon moved away from her and let a waft of frigid air under the covers as he climbed out of bed. He flicked on a bedside lamp, and she received the perfect view of his boxer-clad backside as he bent over to open a drawer. He pulled out a pair of jeans and donned them while Ella stared at his naked back.

When he turned to her, heat suffused her cheeks. Caught in the act.

"Sorry," she blurted. "Your backside is spectacular."

"I will put that on my CV," he said drily. "Stay in bed. I'm going outside to feed Rufus and let out the alpacas to graze. It sounds as if it's still raining."

Ella swallowed and barely resisted tugging the covers over her head. Dillon Williams wasn't bad when he relaxed. She let out a groan once the front door slammed. Her workday started at eight-thirty. She scrambled out of bed and spotted her handbag, right where she'd left it. Perhaps she could get a call through now. She powered up her phone. Nothing. Just perfect. Michael would ask nosy questions. She hadn't informed him of her ghost and the message for Dillon. Actually, she hadn't shared this info with anyone, fearful of them consigning her to Crazy Town.

Unable to go back to sleep, Ella rifled through the pile of clothes Dillon had given her and dressed in a T-shirt, sweatpants and a hoodie. Everything was too big, but she used her dress belt to hold the pants in place and rolled back the hoodie sleeves. A thick pair of socks completed her outfit.

Last night, she had paid little attention to the interior of the house. It was bigger inside than she'd guessed. Bits of wallpaper drooped in places, the pattern screaming of the seventies. Dillon's bedroom appeared freshly decorated, although it held sparse furnishings. The bathroom, too, was modern with a sparkling white-and-chrome shower stall. The white clawfoot tub was positioned to overlook a stand of native trees and the skylight above would offer a great view of the stars on a clear night. Right now, a gray, sullen sky filled the square.

In a continuation of her tour, she poked her nose into the rooms off the passage. One room was full of boxes and furniture. Another seventies fashion statement. The next room was also recently decorated. Cream paint covered three of the walls and teal, gold-and-cream curtains dressed the windows. The fourth wall was one big mural, showing a desert scene and a herd of camels. A discreet signature in the bottom right corner told her Hana Williams had painted the slice of home. A spinning wheel filled one corner, partially woven fleece hanging from the spindle as if the owner had stepped away for a few minutes.

Ella backed out of the room and closed the door. Hana had enjoyed it here. Ella sensed that with every particle of her body. She blinked away the sheen of tears that collected in her eyes. Sorrow and sympathy pressed on her chest. How unfair for Hana to escape the dangers of Afghanistan only to die violently in peaceful New Zealand.

Another doorway led to a lounge still decorated in seventies fashion. A weird mustard-yellow paper covered the walls, although the wear and tear wasn't as bad in this room, which was probably why Dillon and Hana hadn't redecorated this space yet. A huge television hung on one wall while a cozy green two-seater and two single matching green chairs were grouped for perfect viewing.

A framed photo claimed her attention. A smiling, clean-shaven Dillon stood in a casual pose with a petite black-haired woman. Their arms were wrapped around each other, and they appeared relaxed and happy. She'd pictured Hana in her traditional garb, but she wore jeans and a bright red shirt. A beautiful couple.

Ella sighed, envious of their happiness and obvious closeness. This was the reason she'd rejected the two marriage proposals she'd received. While she'd genuinely liked both men, they hadn't made her pulse race. She hadn't wondered about their backsides, ached to touch said buttocks.

A gasp slipped from her, and she clapped her hand over her mouth. She was *not* thinking that way about Dillon Williams.

Ella scurried from the room and found herself in the kitchen. Excellent. Here was something she could do to keep her mind off Dillon. The kitchen held an old pitted countertop and another homage to the seventies in the boxy red cabinets. The pantry was large and well-stocked. She discovered a caddy full of tea bags and a teapot sat near the sink. With the jug filled and on to boil—thank goodness, they still had power—she turned to the fridge. She opened it and discovered at least a dozen plastic containers of food. A loaf of bread. Plenty of milk. A tub of spreadable butter. Bacon. Score! She'd spotted a tray of eggs in the pantry during her search for tea.

A rectangular-shaped wooden table sat at the far end of the spacious kitchen; Dillon must use this for eating his meals since she hadn't spotted a dining room during her explorations. Ella got on with making a pot of tea, cooking the bacon and setting the table.

Halfway through her first cup of tea, she lifted her head at a noise. "Are you ready for breakfast?" she called.

Dillon appeared in the kitchen doorway, his nostrils flaring as he sniffed the air. "You've cooked breakfast?"

She rolled her eyes. "Do you want to eat now? How many eggs? Two or three?"

"Two is fine. I'll wash up."

"Do you take milk in your tea?"

"Please."

He disappeared, and she shook her head, mostly to shake sense into her loopy brain. She was here because of necessity. This wasn't a social call, a booty call or any other call. Dillon was being a good neighbor.

The pipes clanked, the thumps echoing in the walls, and she bustled to the kitchen counter. She cracked three eggs into the hot pan and removed two heated plates from the oven. Dillon entered the kitchen as she placed the crispy bacon on the table. She popped four slices of bread in the toaster.

"Here's your tea," she said, gesturing with her egg slice. "How do you want your eggs?"

"Any way is fine." He grabbed his tea and took a sip. "You don't have to cook for me."

"You didn't need to share your bed," she retorted. "House. I mean, you didn't need to let me stay at your house."

He grinned. "You should stop talking now."

"Yes," she agreed, unable to meet his gaze. Talk about mortifying. She put her mouth in gear and it took off on her. With blazing cheeks, she placed a plate with two eggs

28

in front of him. The toaster clunked, announcing its task done, and she was glad of the opportunity to retreat. A short respite. She delivered the toast then turned off the heat under the frying pan, placed her single egg on a plate and joined Dillon.

"I rarely bother with breakfast."

"I'm starving." Ella buttered a slice of toast and maneuvered her egg until it sat on top of the bread. "If I don't get food and a cup of tea in the morning, I'm a bear."

"You enjoy food."

Ella paused, a piece of bacon hovering in front of her mouth. "Are you calling me fat, Dillon Williams?"

"Where did you get that from?" he demanded. "I never said the F-word. Lighten up, Ella Double-barrel Name." He shunted the toast rack in her direction after taking a slice for himself. "Have more toast and tame that bear."

"Sorry," she mumbled.

He cupped his mug and sipped his tea, eyeing her over the top. "Your body weight is in proportion to your height. You appear healthy. That is what matters."

When she opened her mouth, he lifted his right hand in a stop motion.

Button it, Ella. She wasn't fat. She knew it, but she wasn't skinny either. A touchy subject since the last guy she'd dated had dumped her for someone thinner after telling her she needed to diet. Luckily, the guy who had asked her out tonight had told her he couldn't believe his friend's idiocy. He'd scored an instant date acceptance, after that statement, which reminded her.

"You said you have a satellite phone. I need to ring my

boss and I want to cancel my date with Michael."

"Michael Downing?"

"Have you met him?"

"We attended school together and played rugby for the same team. How long have you been going out with Michael?"

"This will be our first date. I dated Jamie Austin for a few months."

Dillon's mug hovered, his blue eyes watchful. "He prefers his women thin."

"Yes." Even though she aimed for casual, the word emerged crisp and clipped with a side of pissed.

"Ah. Now I get it. Guy's a dickhead, Ella. I'll grab the phone as soon as we're finished eating. Have you tried emailing? For some weird reason, an email will often get through when a phone call won't."

Ella pulled out her phone and tapped an email out, explaining her dilemma. It sent the first time. "I don't have Michael's email."

Dillon ate his last bit of egg and set his knife and fork across the center of his plate. "I'll grab the phone now. When the rain stops, I'll check on the landslide."

"Can I come with you? Do you have a spade or a shovel? I had no tools otherwise I would've tried to dig out my car. Talk about creepy walking in the dark. A working car would've saved me from the bogeyman."

He rolled his eyes and chewed the last corner of his toast.

"What? I'm a scaredy-cat."

Five minutes later, they did the dishes together and took care of the phone calls.

"Your coat is soaked. It's hanging in the laundry room," Dillon said. "I have a selection of raincoats in there. Choose one to wear. It's cold outside."

Ella grabbed a blue coat and rolled the sleeves before she donned the garment and zipped it against the winter chill.

"You ready?"

"Yes."

"Take a hat as well." Dillon slapped a woolen beanie on top of her head before she could reply.

"I resemble the roly-poly tire man."

"You'll be dry and warm. That's all that counts," Dillon said firmly and led the way out the door.

The drive to the spot where she'd left her car took five minutes. Dillon parked and cursed. Ella wanted to parrot his pithy oath, but buttoned her lips and stared at the carnage.

At least half a dozen trees mixed in with the wall of sludgy dirt and tufts of grass. The mountainous pile of debris covered the road—an impossible obstacle to walkers and drivers. With the steep, scarred hill above and the turbulent creek below the road, the trip to Eketahuna would not happen today.

"Where is my car?" Ella asked in a faint voice.

"You're bloody lucky you had the sense to walk to my place," Dillon said, eyeing the barrier. "I didn't think it would be this bad."

3

TRAPPED

PART OF DILLON THOUGHT Ella might have exaggerated about the landslide. She hadn't. Not one bit. In fact, she was lucky to have survived. With the amount of rain they'd had, not even the few remaining trees had held the ground in place.

"I told Dad I'd ring with details. I'd thought we might walk out to get you home. That won't happen. We're trapped, at least until the rain stops and the creek level subsides. Don't get too close in case the hill goes again. The big tree balancing there is a worry."

"My car is under that."

"Is it insured?"

"Yes, but my car has vanished. What happens if the insurance company doesn't believe me?"

"Give Dad your details. We'll get him to notify them and the cops to make things official. Don't worry. They'll find your car when they clear the road."

Dillon noticed Ella trembling while shock had stripped the color from her cheeks. Without considering, he slipped his arm around her waist and drew her against his chest. "It will be all right."

"But I can't stay here indefinitely."

"Not even with my superior backside to ogle?"

"You won't let me forget that, will you?"

"Nope." He approved of her regained color, so he continued his teasing. "You wait until I tell Josh and Summer."

"Your brother and sister?"

He nodded. "Josh will hoot and dispute the fact while Summer will tell me Nikolai has a superior butt. My brother-in-law is in the army too, although he's in training these days rather than on active duty."

"Your family is close. I miss that. I miss my parents."

"What happened?"

"They were in a motor vehicle accident. A head-on crash during a violent storm. They both died at the scene."

"I'm sorry."

Ella shook off her sorrow. "I'm not alone. I have lots of friends. A family of *my* choosing."

"True," Dillon agreed. "My army buddies are my second family."

Dillon explored the ground by the creek and noted exit points. While a vehicle couldn't pass, a person walking might once the level of the creek returned to normal. He retraced his footsteps.

"What will we do now?"

"We'll make more phone calls and sit tight."

"I'm not good at sitting still," Ella said.

"I can always set you to work." Dillon thought she'd protest, but instead, she brightened.

"Perfect. I have my e-reader, but I've almost finished this month's read for the book club."

"What is your book this month?" Curiosity prompted him to ask.

"A romance. We take turns choosing books." Her cheeks turned pink, increasing his interest.

"Should I be checking out this book along with the one about body language? I have an app on my phone for reading."

"I doubt you require any sex tips," she said, her prim tone making him want to smile.

"You know nothing of my experience or techniques." His lips quivered, but his beard covered the evidence.

"We are changing the subject," she stated. "Are you renovating each room of your house? I noticed you've stripped some of the kitchen wallpaper. Are you painting or papering once the surface is prepared? I'm excellent at both."

"I have paint. It won't take me much longer to finish. It will rain again, so that's the perfect job to keep us busy."

"I could make scones for lunch. You have the ingredients."

Dillon opened the vehicle door for her. "I do?"

"Yep, I was nosy this morning. I explored your kitchen. Actually, most of your house."

A laugh escaped him as he shut the door and rounded

the hood. He climbed behind the wheel. "Are you always this honest?"

"I try to be. I loathe liars and try not to commit the crime myself."

"Fair enough."

"What about you?"

Dillon paused. "I tell the truth when it counts, but sometimes my job involves subterfuge." He left it at that, long-formed habits keeping him succinct yet away from telling details. Ella surprised him by not pushing, and he realized he enjoyed her company—even if she did believe in ghosts. In fact, speaking with a neutral person about everyday stuff was helping to still his inner turmoil.

"Do you think the farmer who owns this land could've saved it if he'd left more trees?"

Dillon flicked his gaze over the mountain of wet dirt and plants. "John Donovan owns this land. He didn't clear the trees. I'd say his father or grandfather did the damage. Probably both. Farming methods have changed, ideas shifting over the generations. When the first settlers came to the area, they cleared native bush to make pastures for their sheep and cattle. Some of the steeper land is better left in a natural state."

"You have paddocks."

"We do, but I'm raising alpacas that can handle the hilly country."

"I noticed you've planted trees."

"To attract more birds." His throat closed and he concentrated on driving. It hurt to talk about Hana and the ever-present guilt charged through his mind. A diversion required. "What do you do apart from the book club?"

"I work at Pukaha Mt. Bruce. I adore my job. It's why I moved to Eketahuna. Each day is different and I get to work with the birds. I meet lots of people."

"What is your favorite part?"

"Hmmm." Ella tapped her fingers on her knee and pursed her lips.

She was kinda cute, and he found himself curious to learn more.

"It's difficult to say. The native eels are amazing, and I help with the kiwis sometimes, but working in the shop is fun because I meet travelers from all over the world."

"Why do you dye your hair pink?"

Ella laughed, and the musical sound soothed his tight chest and pushed away the lingering guilt that came from recalling Hana's senseless death.

"Some weeks my hair is blue or turquoise or whatever color I favor on the day. My mother always encouraged me to express myself, and this is one way I chose. Don't you like it?" She pursed her lips, her gaze on him. "It can't be that weighty a decision. A simple yes or no will suffice."

Dillon started, realizing he'd taken his eyes off to road to stare at her lips. Luckily, he'd been driving slowly to suit the conditions. He focused on his driving, but his mind kept drifting. Some people might find her mouth too big, but her plump, pink lips gave a man ideas. "I thought it was weird at first, but it's grown on me." How he got out the words without choking, he had no idea. His dick stirred, and he was glad of his coat. He gripped the steering wheel and sought another topic. "Do you enjoy living in Eketahuna? My sister couldn't wait to escape and spread her wings."

"Some people might say rural towns are dying in New Zealand, but there is a real sense of community here. People are friendly and watch out for each other. I like that. I do a lot of handicrafts in my spare time, go to watch the local rugby team. There are galas and other fund-raising activities."

In other words, she was a woman his mother would approve of and love to have as a daughter-in-law. "How did my mother react when you rang her looking for me?"

"She was helpful."

"In a matchmaking way?"

"Um, yes. But I told her I have a date with Michael."

Dillon suppressed a scowl. He knew his mother and the way her mind worked. Now that Summer was married with a son, their mother had ample time to concentrate on him and Josh.

Dillon pulled up in front of the gate at the foot of his driveway.

"I'll get the gate." Ella was out of his vehicle before he could argue.

He grinned as she splashed through the puddles and yanked on the gate, a blob of layered clothing. During her first visit, she'd worn her coat, the wind whipping her dress to showcase her shapely legs. Curiosity had him craving another peek.

Hell! What the heck was he doing? She was dating Michael and he was returning to Afghanistan. Besides, she

37

wasn't his type. He preferred petite dark-haired women. Women more like Hana even though he and his wife had never been more than just friends. In time, he'd hoped their friendship might deepen to a real marriage, but the home invaders had ripped that opportunity from them.

Ella made waving motions. Bloody hell. And now he was zoning out when he needed to concentrate. He drove through and waited while Ella shut the gate.

"Were you daydreaming?" she demanded as she climbed back into his vehicle.

"No."

Her quizzical expression would've prompted most people to spill. Not him. "You want a cup of tea before we start stripping wallpaper? That's if you still want to help."

"Sure." She glanced at her watch then at him in clear surprise. "Eleven o'clock."

"It took a while to check out the road."

"The time flew."

"You were busy stressing over your car," he said lightly. The truth—her paleness and blank stare had concerned him. The exercise had prodded her awake and out of her introspection.

"I'm hungry. I'll make the scones straight away."

Dillon hid his smile and refrained from mentioning her enjoyment of food. Let no one say he didn't learn from his mistakes. "As long as you don't impede my paper stripping."

"Never," she said in a husky voice. "When are you going to fix the potholes in your driveway?"

"It's on the list. No point doing anything in this

weather."

She nodded. "Makes sense. How many alpacas do you have?"

"Six at present. I'm working on improving the fencing before I increase my flock. I'll wait until I retire though. Dad has to look after them whenever I'm away, and he has enough to do on his farm."

"You could hire someone."

"I tried that, but my employee walked off the job after three weeks. It's difficult finding the right person and keeping an eye on them when I'm half a world away is impossible. Dad still had to come and check, so he told me he'd put it on his list."

"They wouldn't need checking every day."

"No, my girls are self-sufficient."

Ella snorted. "I refuse to comment."

Dillon grinned, the action more natural than it had been in the previous weeks. "I'll let Rufus out for a run. Won't be long."

By the time Dillon reached the kitchen, Ella had the oven heating and the scones underway.

"Who taught you to cook?"

"My auntie. Mum couldn't boil water without a mishap. My learning to cook was self-defense."

"Did you end up cooking dinner?"

"Most of the time, although it never bothered me because that way we had what I wanted to eat. I enjoy curry and lentils, dishes with spice and fragrance. Things with a hint of heat but not too much to make your eyes water."

"The food in Afghanistan is similar to Indian and

Pakistani meals, but they don't use as many spices. Have you traveled?"

"I've seen the North Island, and we had family vacations on the Gold Coast of Australia and Fiji. I'd love to travel more. I suppose you've visited more countries."

Dillon shrugged. "The hot spots, although we've done joint training exercises with the Australian and British forces. We don't get much downtime to explore." He grabbed his paper-stripping tool and set to work.

Soon the scent of scones filled the kitchen. Cheese scones, Ella had informed him since they were her favorite. His lips twitched as he watched her bustle around his kitchen.

"You have soup," she announced. "We'll have it for lunch."

"Mum and the local ladies have stocked my fridge even though I'm capable of looking after myself."

"Did you tell them that?"

"Mum likes having one of her brood at home to fuss over. The other women have...had an agenda."

"They were after your luscious body," Ella said.

"I...what?" Dillon glanced over his shoulder in time to catch her wink. "You looking at my arse again?"

"Maybe."

Unexpected heat collected in Dillon's cheeks, so he returned to stripping paper. He preferred to place his women in boxes, keeping them separate from the important things in his life. His friends and fellow soldiers. His work. Ella's artlessness was throwing him off his game, and somehow, she'd dispersed his normal gruffness.

"The paint won't dry well in this weather."

"It won't matter. I'll do this one wall and open the windows when I can to let out the paint fumes. I'm not in a hurry to finish."

"How long have you had the property?"

"Six years now. Not much time to spend my money when I'm working. I wanted to have something for the future."

"That's very forward-thinking of you."

Dillon worked on removing the last strip of wallpaper. The truth was he'd purchased the block of land on a whim, borrowing from his parents to complete the sale. Since then, he'd repaid their loan. A place of his own had worked for him and Hana, and since his return on leave, the property had been a place to hide while he sorted out his head.

His satellite phone rang, and he set down his scraper to answer the call.

"Mum," he said.

"Do you like, Ella? She's such a lovely girl. I thought you'd hit it off together."

"Mum, stop. Ella is nice, but she's dating Michael."

Ella's head jerked and she stared at him with head-lamp eyes. She made him want to laugh.

"Pooh, Michael. You could win her away without breaking a sweat."

"I'm going outside," he said to Ella. Three long strides later, he was out the front door and standing in the unused carport. "Mum, stop. Hana died six months ago. It is way too early to romance another woman."

"You have needs," his mother said, unrepentant.

"I can tell Nikolai, with my hand on my heart, that Summer isn't an original. She inherited her outrageousness from you," Dillon snapped. "Butt out, Mum. Ella is dating Michael, who I happen to respect."

"Where is she sleeping?"

No missing the slyness in that query. His mother was in full matchmaking mode. "On the couch."

"Dillon Jason Williams! I raised you better than that."

Dillon held the phone farther from his ear. "I'm an adult, Ma," he snapped, knowing the *Ma* would irritate her. "What I do in my home is my business. Not yours. Not anyone else's. Stop matchmaking because it will not happen. I'm heading back to Afghanistan at the end of September."

"I understand." His mother sounded subdued now. "I'm sorry, Dillon. I want you to be happy again."

Dillon sighed. "Mum, you can't expect me to jump straight into another relationship. What if something happened to Dad? Would you remarry within six months?"

"No, you're right. Dillon, I'm sorry. It's just Ella is a lovely girl. She is popular."

"Yeah, Michael has excellent taste. Gotta go. Lunch is ready."

"Do you need anything?"

"No, we have stacks of food. The creek is too high to skirt the landslide at present. As long as the rain eases, we should get Ella out in two days."

"This rain is a nuisance."

"It's still winter. I'll ring when we're ready to walk out and Dad can meet us on the other side. One more thing—Ella will need a vehicle. Are you using Hana's car?"

"Excellent idea, son. We'll make sure the car is running. Take care. Oh, and Dillon?"

"Yes?"

"You're a tough soldier, used to sleeping on the ground. Let Ella have the bed."

Before he could reply, the line clicked in his ear. His mother had hung up after having the last word. Typical.

The afternoon passed in easy companionship. They started painting the kitchen. Ella helped him return the alpacas to shelter for the night. Later, they heated one of the casseroles from his fridge and ate it along with mashed potatoes. They watched a movie together and nibbled on shortbread that Ella had baked at the same time as her scones. The girl had kitchen skills.

"You take the bed," Ella said once the movie ended. "I can fit on the couch."

"I don't mind sharing my bed."

"No," Ella said promptly enough to wound his male ego.

In the end, he caved. "There are spare blankets in the hall cupboard." He collected them for her and left her to it, all the while forcing sex out of his brain. Funny, but he hadn't had that problem for a while, hadn't missed sex while he'd been with Hana.

One day with Ella, and it was all he could think about.

4

EVENING SHENANIGANS

THE ICY COLD WOKE Ella. Disoriented, because the subtle glow of her nightlight wasn't present, she shivered beneath the weight of three heavy blankets. She peered through the absolute darkness, frowning until she recalled she was sleeping on the couch. The too-short couch, she'd discovered during her first stretch. The fire no longer burned in the hearth, and desperate for warmth, she decided she'd crawl into Dillon's bed. After all, he'd surprised her by doing the same.

It wasn't that she had designs on his muscular body.

She scowled.

Well, maybe she did.

A woman wasn't alive if she didn't look at Dillon Williams and wonder exactly how hard those muscles would bounce against her fingertips. What sort of lover he'd be? Not even that wild, bushy beard of his was enough to put her off now that she'd spent the day with him and peeled away the first of his layers.

But she had restraint.

She wasn't a cavewoman intent on clubbing her competitors to win the man with the best forward propulsion.

No, she was not.

Contrasting warmth and cold battled within her body, and she attempted to refocus.

Unfortunately, now that the topic of sex filled her mind, it was difficult to find a replacement thought. She plain liked Dillon and enjoyed his company.

And dating Michael...

She sighed, aware of the uncomfortable conversation that lay in her future when Dillon kept intruding and producing wicked notions. Ella stood and let out a yelp.

The icy floor dampened her lust, and she fumbled for her socks. Ugh! Still cold. She bumbled her way around the two-seater and the two other chairs. The door creaked when she opened it, and she blundered into a wall since the passage was as black as Hades. Once she found the wall, she progressed more steadily to Dillon's bedroom.

In the doorway, she paused, peering through the darkness. Dillon lay on the left side of the bed, his breathing normal.

Why the devil didn't he snore? The man must have one or two imperfections.

Ella inched closer, more confident now. She supposed his beard rated as a minus although he probably considered it a deterrent to his female visitors. He should stop bathing if he wanted to drive off unwanted guests. That was one thing women agreed on—cleanliness in a man. She'd suggest it to him tomorrow. No, today because surely it was after midnight by now.

Finally, she reached the bed and made her way stealthily to the right side. She pulled back the covers and...

A scream rang out, echoing in the bedroom.

Hers.

A heavy mass pinned her to the bed. She couldn't move. She could barely gather enough breath for another screech of protest.

"Ella?" a hoarse voice demanded.

A lamp switched on, but the weight of a man on her chest never lessened.

She blinked as she stared at Dillon's fierce visage. His soldier face. At least, that was her assumption. Determination and bold power radiated from his eyes. Her gaze drifted downward, and she swallowed.

"Where are your clothes?"

"Why are you creeping into my bedroom?" Dillon countered.

Ella ripped her gaze off his broad chest and noticed a faint scar on his shoulder. Her gaze drifted lower, and her eyes widened. He had a six-pack. No, make that an eight-pack. Lots of packs. And he'd ditched the tight-fitting boxers. The man had an all-over tan. How did he manage that in the middle of winter? Surely... No, she gathered Afghanistan was a conservative country. She doubted any of the soldiers ran around naked.

"Ella." Her name held a warning. Explain or else.

"Um, yes?" Something tempted her to learn what the *or else* might be.

"What are you doing here?" He added a growl. A dark, sexy rumble that made her fingers flex in the sheets.

"Well…" Her gaze wandered his muscles.

"Were you waiting for me to relax before you made your move?"

"No! Jeesh! What is it with you Eketahuna men? You have high opinions of yourself and consider you're God's greatest gift to the female species. I was cold because the fire has gone out. The couch is too short, and I couldn't stretch out with comfort. Three blankets aren't keeping me warm. How was I meant to know you were naked in here? I mean, what sort of idiot strips to the buff in this icy weather? It's inhuman. Nuts! Cray-cray. Definitely cray-cray."

"Push the off button, Ella Double-barrel Name." His lips pursed, and she received a brief flash of white teeth. "Do I make you nervous?"

"Yes. No!"

"Which is it?"

"I didn't expect golden muscles to hit me when I got into bed. Nakedness. Can you get off me now? Eek! Why do you have an erection? It's too cold. I thought icy temperatures killed erections?"

Dillon barked out a laugh. "Apparently not."

"Well, put it away. Too much naked male splendor might induce me to deliver casseroles and cupcakes. Don't forget, I'll be party to the secret way around the blocked road. A landslide won't stop me. Hell, no!" Why couldn't she stop this verbal diarrhea? She pressed her lips together and held her breath. Why did he smell so good? "If you pelted the casserole ladies with body odor instead of citrus and manly musk, you'd have more hope of them fleeing. Stop taking showers. That should do it. No woman is attracted to a stinky man."

Dillon stared at her with his baby-blues.

Ella swallowed, unwilling to break their visual connection. The silence stretched way past uncomfortable. She broke first, her gaze darting downward over the expanse of golden muscles to land on his groin. She gasped.

"You should trim your beard. I could do that for you tomorrow. You're safe from the casserole ladies for a while—at least until they clear the road—so you should tidy that facial hair. You don't want to scare your alpacas. I'll help you trim it tomorrow."

Dillon's eyes glowed. Was that heat in his gaze? She thought it might be, and her pulse raced even faster. Her heart thumped. *Bang. Bang. Bang.*

"There is one sure-fire way to silence you."

She blinked and stiffened as her mind followed his words. "Ah, I might be warmer now. I'll...um...go back to the couch. Yes, that's an excellent idea. Much safer."

"Why?"

"Because I'm considering jumping you. I haven't had sex for a long time, and it's a shame to waste a good erection."

There was one of those pregnant pauses, and this time Dillon blinked. Ella's heartbeat banged a fraction harder, a fraction louder while heat crawled from her cheeks, down her neck to tickle her breasts.

She refrained from squirming.

Just.

"If you won't shut up, I'll have to make you." An instant later, Dillon's mouth covered hers.

The *oomph* burst out of her urge to flee, and she froze.

Dillon smiled against her lips before he rearranged his big body for comfort, wrapped his arms around her and settled in to kiss her properly. Soft lips caressed hers. Teasing yet not hesitant. He used firm pressure. Perfect pressure while keeping the kiss on the right side of innocent. Just as she relaxed, he upped his game. Oh yes. The man had technical skills. His tongue coaxed her to open to him, and when she did, he took immediate advantage. Their tongues slid together in a sensual dance that sent flares of delight southward.

She moaned against his mouth and wound her arms around his neck to hold him tight in case he ended this decadent treat.

Thankfully, he continued to kiss her, exhibiting a wide knowledge and experience that she made a mental note to ask about later. His kissing skills—sublime. Inspirational compared to the more recent efforts she'd experienced.

Her body sizzled with an urgent desire, a low prickling heat building between her legs. Her breasts grew swollen and heavy as she relaxed in his arms.

Finally, he lifted his head, and she groaned her disappointment.

"Are you stopping?"

She received a flash of a grin as he moved away from her aching body. He switched off the lamp, and the covers rustled as he situated himself.

Ella sighed. He'd ruined her for kissing other men. Not that she intended to tell him that. She turned over onto her side and faced away from him. Best not to let him decide she was angling for more. She'd hate him to think less of her, and she hadn't come to his bedroom for this. Getting warmer had been her priority, and she'd aced that.

A muscular arm curled around her waist, and she jumped.

"Are you tired of kissing me?"

"Um, no." *That was an embarrassing squeak.*

"Good," he said. "Because now I've thought about sex, I can't stop."

Before she could question him, he'd turned her back to face him and his lips against hers put a halt on information gathering.

That prickle of heat flared to life again, and she ached to have his hands on her breasts. Yet asking for this would mean he'd have to remove his lips from hers. That wouldn't do at all. Mouths met, teased, brushed. Tongues twirled and danced.

Dillon parted their mouths. "I'm at a disadvantage here. You should remove your shirt to even the stakes. Opinion?"

"Ah, yes?" Where was that annoying squeak coming from? She cleared her throat. "Yes, please."

Frigid air struck her upper torso as he tossed the blankets aside. He helped her rise and removed her T-shirt with expertise that made her blink. Nothing wrong with his seductive skills. What on earth did they teach them in soldier school?

Dillon gently pushed her back onto the mattress. He rearranged the covers and used himself as a human blanket. Warmth seared her naked breasts.

"Much better." Dillon kissed her while his big, warm hand coasted along her triceps. His fingers unerringly found one breast. Proof that a man was quite capable of multitasking. A shiver ran through Ella. It streaked from her mouth to her breast and down the highway of her body, straight to her clit. Sexual excitement propelled damp arousal even though common sense told her that this could go nowhere.

Dillon was a widower who'd recently lost his wife. He was a soldier and a career one at that. Ella allowed her hands to wander in return. She mightn't get another chance to explore these glorious muscles. Her fingertips skimmed the planes of his back, and daring made her let them drift even lower until they settled on his tight backside. He clenched for an instant, and Ella wasn't sure if she'd surprised him or if he was showing off. Either way, she now had firsthand experience and could say she never doubted his ability to propel sperm.

The thought gave her pause.

Birth control.

If they ever got that far, they were in trouble. She wasn't on birth control. Disappointment filled her since now that she'd allowed herself to daydream and ponder, she'd love to examine his cock with closer attention.

His big hand settled over her breast, then he moved down her body and before she could utter a word, his lips drew on her nipple. A loud moan of enjoyment escaped her, and instantly, heat filled her cheeks.

Heck. Just call her easy. Call her desperate. Call her seduced.

She'd always enjoyed a man's mouth on her breasts, and this man had moves.

His mouth tugged her nipple as he released it. "You like that."

No point in denial. "Yes."

"How far do you want us to take this?" His fingers toyed with her nipple, making it difficult for her to focus.

"I...ah...um... Will you stop that for a moment? I can't concentrate."

He chuckled.

"Ah...if I told you I want more would you lump me in with the Casserole Ladies? Because I didn't come here for sex. But now that I'm in your bed and half-naked, I might cry if we stop."

His fingers tightened on her breast, and she sighed her enjoyment, savored the spike of heat in her pussy.

"I haven't done this for a while," she confessed. "That's not helping clear thought processes."

He laughed again. "Are you on birth control?"

"No." Regret tinged her reply.

"I have condoms somewhere. Possibly in the drawer on your side."

"Do you want to use one?"

"More like two or three," Dillon said. "What do you say

about that?"

"Yes. Although I'm sure you have excellent forward propulsion, as evidenced by your spectacular arse, I'm not ready for children."

He laughed. "You crack me up." He reached over her and pulled out a bedside drawer. He mumbled then moved to turn on the bedside lamp again. "Ah, that's better."

Ella gaped at the monster pack of condoms. "You go for the jumbo pack."

"I didn't buy this. My sister and Nikolai gave both me and Josh these for Christmas. It's a joke since my brother and I walked in on Summer and Nikolai one day. There were condoms all over the floor and things got a mite heated because she's our baby sister and we didn't approve of Nikolai."

"Do you like your sister's husband now?"

"He's grown on us," Dillon said. "He's great with my sister and their son." As he spoke, he opened a brand-new variety pack from the Fancy Free condom company. "One of Nikolai and Summer's friends lives in Sloan where they make these condoms. Sorrel, his wife, works for Fancy Free."

"You have interesting friends."

"I'm more interested in you right now. Want to take off the rest of your clothes?"

Ella nibbled her bottom lip. "I suppose I could brave the cold for you."

"I'll make you warm. Promise. Besides, I'd like to check out your backside."

"That's a terrible idea."

"Why?"

"I'm positive mine won't measure up to yours."

"Let me be the judge of that." He kissed the tip of her nose and tossed back the rest of the covers. Cold air frisked her skin as Dillon tugged on her borrowed pajama pants.

The silence bothered her, so she filled it. "You've done this before."

"Yes." Wary blue eyes studied her face. "You have too."

"Good point." He had her there.

"What are you trying to say?"

"Just that you're competent at undressing a woman."

"Pajama pants and a T-shirt don't require skill." His eyes twinkled. "Although if you were wearing a bra that might present a challenge. But, I have to say, I'm more than competent in that arena."

"Smartarse."

"I could say the same about you."

Ella sniffed and tried not to communicate her amusement. This man kept her off-balance. He reduced her to babble and she careened out of control with no way to put the brakes on her wayward emotions. After their short acquaintance, she was willingly jumping into bed with him. Object: sex, pleasure and hopefully fun.

"Aren't you going to take off my socks?"

"I thought you might have cold feet."

Ella sniffed again. "Naked people wearing socks look ridiculous. There should be a rule that it's not allowed." She peered at him more closely. "Do you break the sock rule? Consider carefully because this is a deal breaker for me."

He chuckled. "I always sleep naked unless I'm camping in the great outdoors and need to move in a hurry."

"Excellent. Socks. Off, please."

He slid off her socks then aligned their bodies and pulled the covers over them. Heat radiated off his big body while she shivered and worked to keep her teeth from chattering.

"Now where were we?" he asked.

"Kissing. Touching. Smooching. In that order."

"The caresses have been one-sided thus far. Just saying."

Ella stared, trying to read his expression. Difficult since the man resembled a blank slate. "Is that a dare? Because if it is, I accept. I respond well to challenges."

Dillon flopped over on his back and placed his hands behind his head. His pectoral muscles shifted as he moved, attracting her avid attention. "If staring is all you've got, you're heading for an F grade."

An inelegant snort escaped her, and she rolled her eyes for emphasis. If she wasn't looking forward to this treat so much she'd pinch his splendid muscular backside. No, the wretch would enjoy that too much.

"Prepare to suffer." She made spider motions in the air and watched him grin. She wished she could read his face. Tomorrow, she'd offer to trim his beard again. He might agree.

His blue eyes glinted in a challenge, but she didn't let his confidence needle her. Instead, she straddled his body and leaned over him. His swift intake of breath and his avid attention as her breasts neared his face told her she had his complete cooperation. This was gonna be fun.

She licked on a flat nipple, stroking the disk with her

tongue while her hands got busy with his shoulders. Strong shoulders. His scent washed over her. There were citrus notes and a hint of something green. His soap or shampoo or that surprising bottle of body wash she'd noted on a shelf in the shower. Her fingers tiptoed over his biceps, which bunched on contact. Oh, he was trying to remain still and not react to her teasing strokes but deniability wasn't working from his end.

Now, the ultimate test. She slid back a fraction, her backside coming into contact with his erection. She wriggled back and forward and gloried in his gasp. Ha! She'd guessed right. His impassiveness was a front and this big, bad SAS man felt things deeply. A case in point—the way he fell silent whenever his wife's name came up.

Ella stilled.

She didn't want to hurt him or get hurt herself. Maybe she should walk away before things progressed any further. Then, she admitted the truth. While she didn't believe in love at first sight, the building blocks of a serious relationship were already cemented in her mind.

"Hey," he said. "Having second thoughts?"

"I don't wish to get hurt. When I fall for a guy, I usually fall hard." There she went with that honesty again.

"We've only met. I intend to rejoin my team."

"Yes. I get that. I'm not the woman who jumps into bed with a man on the first date."

"We can stop. I have capable hands. I won't die from blue balls."

"No, you don't understand. For the first time that's not a problem for me."

"We don't have a future together." Blunt and ringing with honesty.

"I understand. Could we be friends with benefits while you're here? And the next time you come home, we can reassess if we're still on the same page? We can make a list of rules."

"Number one. My mother must never find out about us," he said.

"Pep-talk done. Let's hash out the rules tomorrow."

He offered her his hand to seal the deal. A spark of electricity jumped up her arm, and she barely held back a gasp.

"Can we stop talking now?"

His plaintive tone made her laugh.

"I like you Dillon Williams and I hereby agree to friends with benefits, the finer points to be hashed out tomorrow."

"Deal, Ella Liddington-Walsh."

She grinned. "Where is that box of condoms? I want to get to the good stuff now."

Dillon reached for the box and ripped it open. He separated one condom and tossed the box and the rest of the strip on the bedside cabinet.

Ella scooted off Dillon and opened the foil packet. She rolled the condom onto his shaft without a fumble.

"You've done that before."

"My girlfriends and I used to practice on a wooden phallus. We decided the skill might come in handy."

"That's scary."

"No different from guys practicing to unhook a bra. I

57

bet you and your mates did that when you were younger."

"Nope, my talent comes naturally."

Ella sniggered. "Whatever."

"I'm taking control since you've squandered your opportunity."

He reacted so quickly she'd barely formulated a protest, let alone voiced it. Ella found herself staring at him, blinking at the intensity radiating from his gaze. His callused hands cupped her breasts and toyed with her nipples. Sometimes soft. Sometimes hard. Always pleasurable. He kissed her again with his skillful mouth and soon she drifted, his strokes and caresses making her body sing.

He moved his attention lower, working down her torso. His tongue rimmed her bellybutton while his callused hands curved around her hipbones. Her breathing grew faster and her pulse raced.

His fingers stroked her slit and the burst of pleasure had her gasping aloud. He chuckled at her reaction, but she didn't take offense. His skillful fingers worked in a pleasing rhythm that told her he wasn't boasting about his experience. Either he'd done this a lot, or he'd learned from an excellent teacher.

She. Didn't. Care.

Friends with benefits. It was official. No jealousy here. Instinct told her if the green-eyed monster got hold of her, this would turn into a one-hit wonder.

Greedily, she wanted much more.

Dillon lifted her to his mouth. His tongue finessed her clit with light pressure. Perfect pressure. So perfect. The faint prickle forecasting an imminent climax sizzled from the point of contact.

"Dillon." She wriggled, and his head lifted.

"Too much?"

"I'm going to come."

"And that's a problem why?"

"I-I..." Ella frowned.

"If it's any consolation, I won't last long once I get inside you. Take what you can now," he advised with an audacious wink.

"As long as we practice over the next few days and increase our stamina."

He barked out a laugh. "We'll add that to our agreement. Can I go back to licking now?"

"Feel free," she said in an airy voice.

This time, he licked and caressed with a purpose. He slid one long finger into her heat and angled his finger, hitting the perfect spot.

Ella closed her eyes to better enjoy his superior skills. The man...she'd never... Heck, she couldn't wait to experience everything with him. He lifted his mouth for an instant, and she was tempted to grab his ears and redirect him back to her clit.

"Dillon."

He blew warm air over her needy flesh, and a shiver worked through her.

"Please. I'm close. Don't tease me now. And do that finger thing inside me. I like that."

"Yes, ma'am."

"And put away that cocky grin. It's irritating."

Dillon laughed, the exuberant sound making her blink. He'd smiled once he'd warmed to her company, but this wholehearted amusement was new. She promised herself to make it her mission to bring more joy to his life.

Dillon settled to lick her again.

"Perfect," she said. "I love a man who takes direction."

His tongue waggled and a puff of air heated her flesh at the same time. She'd made him laugh or at least smile again. Score.

Then in the next instant, Dillon pushed her toward the edge. She strained, lifting her hips and chasing the elusive orgasm. Seconds later, she shattered with the dual tongue caresses and his finger stroking her deep inside. Pleasure darted along her legs and whisked upward in another wave, frisking her breasts and filling her face with heat. Gradually, she released her tense muscles and Dillon took that as a sign to back away from more stimulation.

"Ah." She sighed with enjoyment. "That was magnificent."

"My turn." He levered his body, positioned his cock at her entrance and pushed inside her with one seamless stroke. "Damn. That is perfect. You okay?"

She nodded even though his length stretched her to the point of discomfort.

He kissed her, sealing their lips together and withdrew. He entered her again with an uncompromising thrust, and this time, his shaft slid more easily, the friction drifting over the border to blissful.

Ella clutched his shoulders, savoring his hard strength as he surrounded her, filled her, dominated her with his need.

Their lips parted, and she nibbled his neck. A dark groan told her he liked that, so she repeated the move, giving him a fraction more teeth.

His strokes became rapid and choppy, his breathing harsh, and she reveled in her power over this strong man. He came with a hoarse groan, his big body stilling balls-deep in her. After a long moment, he kissed her again, this time gentle and short. Despite this, the kiss punched at her psyche, and she reminded herself this was a temporary relationship, meant to benefit them both. If she was stupid enough to fall for him, despite their short acquaintance, more fool her.

5

THE BEARD EPISODE

Dillon left Ella sleeping the next morning. He didn't creep, but he used his soldier training to leave his bedroom without detection. After a quick shower, he padded to the kitchen, his mind stuck on Ella.

He hadn't expected this, hadn't planned it at all, but something about Ella challenged him, made him forget his good intentions. Even though they were new acquaintances, he'd guessed she didn't do casual. The local gossip would've reached his mother. She'd steer Ella away from him if this was the case.

Friends with benefits.

An interesting concept and one that worked for him as long as he didn't let himself get too serious. One-night stands weren't his thing, but if he added friendship to the mix...

Deep in his head, Dillon pulled on a jacket and donned

his gumboots. As he'd expected, the worst of the rain had passed and the sky didn't hold the sullen grayness of the last few days. Native birds sang and twittered in the nearby block of bush, and their happiness pleased him. He and Hana had trapped extensively to rid their corner of introduced pests, and he intended to remain vigilant with possums and rats to keep the bird population healthy.

Once he'd fed and watered Rufus, he checked on his alpacas. He scratched a fuzzy white head and smiled at the other beasts who nudged him for the same attention. With the alpacas fed and wandering around their paddock, he returned to the house, leaving Rufus to run loose.

If Ella wanted, they'd drive to the landslide and check the level of the creek. She had to be sick of wearing borrowed clothes. His grin was wolfish as he recalled her luscious, naked body curled against his. Option number two. Ditch the clothes and return to bed.

Now that one appealed big time.

When he reentered the house, Ella was in the shower. He strode along the passage and banged on the door. "Do you want more clothes?"

"I already found clean clothes," she shouted back. The shower turned off, and the door opened a few seconds later. "I hope you don't mind, but I raided your wardrobe. I'll do the washing today."

He scanned her naked shoulders and her cleavage, the rest hidden by the towel wrapped around her torso. "Tea or coffee?"

"Whatever you're having. What are you making me for breakfast? I'm hungry."

Dillon's lips twitched. "It's a surprise."

By the time Ella arrived in the kitchen, he had a cheese and mushroom omelet underway and a plunger of coffee waiting to pour. Without being asked, Ella set the table and poured coffee for them both.

He shot straight to the meat of his thoughts. "Are we going to discuss rules today?"

"Yes. Where do you hang your laundry when it's raining? Do you have a drier?"

"No drier. I have a line in the carport. The wind whistles through there and it dries fast."

Ella nodded. "Do you have other laundry? I might as well do everything at once."

"You don't have to look after me."

"You babysat me after the landslide. Can I trim your beard?"

"An attempt to fix me?"

"No, I'd prefer to see the shape of your face. Right now, you resemble a mountain man."

"Have you done this before?"

"No."

"And I should trust you why?"

"Because I'm the one who looks at you, and if I make a mess, it will hurt my eyes. Not yours."

Dillon grinned. "Good point." She kept him guessing with her outrageous comments. He never knew what words would fall from her luscious mouth next. "I want to check the boundary fences in case any trees have fallen during the storm. The neighbor has cattle, and I don't want them eating out my paddocks."

"Can I come with you?"

"It will be muddy."

"I have gumboots."

Dillon had wondered if Ella might grow tired of the great outdoors It was muddy and cold, despite the sunshine. Once again, she surprised him. She snapped photos of the trees and came to an abrupt halt when she spotted a gray bird with a bright blue wattle.

"A kokako," she breathed, lifting her phone to take a photo. "We have wild birds on the reserve. It's exciting to learn the population is growing."

"There are a lot of birds. More than there used to be."

A loud *whop-whop* rent the air and Dillon frowned.

"That's a big bird," Ella said as the helicopter flew over their heads and banked right.

"I didn't realize the neighbor had a chopper."

"Perhaps he has a visitor."

"Possible." Dillon realized he'd noticed the helicopter twice since he'd arrived home. He hadn't blinked the first time, but now he wondered why his neighbor—a cattle farmer—had a helicopter. Not a single reason occurred as to why the man owned one, although maybe Ella was right, and the guy's friends or family owned a bird. A helicopter was the perfect vehicle at present with the access road blocked.

"Oh, Dillon." Ella's reverent tone drew his attention. The sun caught her profile as she gazed at him, the rays turning her pink streaks to fiery red. "Look."

She pointed at a set of tracks on the ground. Bird prints, in particular. Three toes with the middle one much longer than the two outside ones. Her eyes blazed with excitement when she glanced at him. "Those look like kiwi tracks to me. I'd love to glimpse a wild kiwi."

"I listen to them at night sometimes if I can't sleep. Once the weather gets better, you might hear them call."

She skipped farther along the trail, eyes down, backside up and reminding Dillon of a dog on a scent. Her arse wasn't so shabby either. His hands tingled, recalling the previous night and the way her curves had nestled into his body. He couldn't wait for a repeat.

She came to an abrupt halt. "Look."

Dillon ambled closer and spotted a series of holes in the bank. Ella had her backside sticking in the air again, and he barely restrained himself.

"I'm sure these are probe marks," Ella said. "I wonder where the kiwi burrow is."

"It could be anywhere around here," Dillon said. "My block backs on to the neighbor's place and your wildlife center. The proximity to Mt. Bruce is part of the reason I have so many native birds in my section of bush. That's my boundary fence there." He gestured, checking the condition of the fence by sight. It didn't look as if any trees had toppled during the storm.

Dillon led the way farther along the track, which exited the trees at a summit.

"You have a beautiful plot of land." Ella stopped beside him, her face glowing with exercise and enthusiasm. "How much are you intending to clear for pasture?"

"I have enough to graze a larger herd of alpaca. Hana and I..." Dillon trailed off, realizing although he thought about Hana, he seldom spoke of her aloud. He cleared his throat and forced himself to continue. "We didn't intend to increase our herd by too much. We figured we had sufficient grazing for at least thirty alpacas. We intended to have a hobby farm rather than a large unit." Dillon stopped talking, his throat tight.

Ella's expression softened as she gazed over the bush, the pastures beyond and the silver glint of the distant creek. "You wanted enough animals for Hana to cope with on her own."

"Yes, with Dad's help. We started small to make sure the area was suitable for the alpacas. They're thriving, and Hana was excited about building the herd numbers."

"You're intending to continue with your plan."

"I like working with the animals. They're friendly and curious. Good natured."

"What will happen when you rejoin your soldier friends?"

"Dad has been looking after them. It's not ideal, but a better solution hasn't presented itself."

"I could look after them for you."

"No," Dillon snapped.

Ella flinched at his spurt of temper. "I—"

"I don't want you here on your own. It's not safe. The fences are fine. Let's head back to the house now."

Ella nodded, quiet after his snappish reply, and another layer of guilt slapped on his shoulders. Then he stiffened and straightened, unrepentant at his harsh words. He'd left Hana here alone and he'd be damned if he placed another woman in the same position, even if it meant battered emotions and an empty bed.

"Well, can I at least buy fleece off you? I'd like to try spinning it."

"There is a bag in storage. I'll deliver it to your place."

"How much will you charge?"

"I don't want your money." And he was snarling again. Dillon sucked in a long breath and eased it out slowly while he struggled with his temper. He paused, realizing he'd stomped with long strides, leaving Ella behind. "Sorry."

Instead of acting snappish in return, Ella reached out and squeezed his arm in silent commiseration. "I'm sorry too. Why don't I trim your beard when we get back? I'd get to view your angry face in its full glory. Earlier, I missed the full effect." And she winked at him.

Dillon's mouth dropped open, and he gaped at Ella. His mouth shut, opened, and clacked shut with finality.

"No comment?"

A growl escaped him, and Ella laughed.

"Maybe we can shower together," she suggested.

Dillon did the fish mouth thing again because words failed him. Instead, he walked in silence. His sat-phone rang, and he answered it with relief.

"Hi, Dad. No, I haven't checked the creek level yet. We're intending to drive down later this afternoon. Yeah. Okay. We should be able to get Ella out tomorrow, as long as it doesn't rain again." He paused, listening to his mother speaking in the background. "No, we're fine for food, but Ella is looking forward to getting home. She's tired of my bad moods."

Ella squeezed his arm again and pulled a face at him.

Some of the emotional weight lifted off his shoulders and he wanted to grin at her. He restrained himself as he told his father he'd ring once he'd checked the water levels.

Back at the house, they drank tea to warm up.

"Do you have scissors or a beard trimmer?" Ella asked. "Ideally both."

"Hana would have scissors," he said. "They'll be in her craft room."

"Is it okay for me to go in there?"

"Sure."

"While I'm gone, put the chair in the light and get a towel to put around your shoulders."

"Yes, ma'am." Dillon watched her sashay from the kitchen, sexy and alluring even in her baggy sweatpants and an overlarge T-shirt.

Ella reappeared minutes later, brandishing two pairs of scissors. "If I make a mess, you can shave the lot off."

Dillon stared at her. "Are you always this cheerful?"

"Mostly. I'm a cup-half-full kind of girl. Life is too short for pessimism and gloom. I like to embrace life and shoot for adventure."

Not a bad way to live. She'd shown this verve for life, and in turn, helped to lift some of his own despondency.

"Let's do this," he said and planted his butt on the chair she indicated.

Ella wrapped the towel around his shoulders then took a step back.

"What are you doing?"

"You need a haircut too. I have experience in that arena."

Something about the quiver of her mouth told him to

ask questions. "Are you any good?"

"My doll's hair never grew back." She chuckled. "You should see your expression right now."

Yet again, Dillon laughed. "Just the beard, thanks."

"Okay." Her humor slid away, and she cocked her head. "Close your eyes. I can't concentrate with those cute baby-blues watching me."

Obediently, he shut his eyes. Her hands cupped his face, and she wielded the scissors. He relaxed since she'd spoken the truth. If he hated the result, he could shave and start on a new beard.

She snipped and hummed and fingered his face. Gradually, heat radiated through him, awareness of Ella creating a need. Her fragrance filled his slow inhalations, and his mind drifted to showering and sex. He huffed out a groan.

"What's wrong?"

"You standing this close is pushing my mind to sex."

"Okay," she said agreeably, doing more snipping. "It will be much nicer kissing you now. You're rocking this beard. You've turned into a handsome dude. I bet your eyes will pop."

"Huh?"

"Shush. Don't move. I'm almost finished." Her hands brushed over his cheeks and chin. "You might need to trim with a razor, but this beard looks good on you."

Dillon opened his eyes as she set the scissors on the counter. He removed the towel from around his shoulders and dropped it on the kitchen floor. Without thought, he grabbed Ella by the hips and dragged her onto his knee. She let out a tiny *eep* of shock but soon relaxed into his embrace. He rubbed his cheek against hers before adjusting the angle and kissing her.

Her lips were soft and clung to his. Their tongues tangled in mutual pleasure.

"Does this new beard pass muster?"

"You're a handsome dude, Dillon Williams. The women will deliver casseroles by helicopter once they get a glimpse of the new you."

"Put it back," Dillon said. "Those casserole ladies are scary."

She smoothed her hand over his chin. "Too late, buster."

The *whop-whop* of the helicopter sounded, coming closer. Dillon frowned, wondering why the pilot would circle his house. He stood, his hands on Ella's hips until she gained her balance. The helicopter passed overhead and flew toward Palmerston North. Dillon studied the navy-blue bird through the window, unsettled by something in his gut that told him this was unusual. In all his time here with Hana, he'd never spotted one helicopter.

His neighbor might be organizing the spraying of noxious weeds or using the chopper for another reason. Something innocent. Yet Dillon's gut said otherwise, and he had no explanation for his instincts. Once Ella left, he promised himself he'd do a little investigation. At the least, it was an opportunity to practice his soldiering skills.

He turned away from the window. "I'm off to find a mirror in case you're talking up abysmal shaving skills. Are you ready for that shower?"

Ella couldn't believe how fast the day disappeared and how much she'd enjoyed spending time with Dillon. She hadn't been kidding about his appearance. Her heart did an extra blip each time she glanced at him. Now, she witnessed his expressions, although the man possessed impassive skills she'd never break.

Dillon didn't scare her though. She'd glimpsed his marshmallow inside and experienced his kindness, and then there was the lovemaking. She was certain he'd spoiled her for other men. Michael... She sighed. She'd have to tell him she was only interested in being friends. She'd thought there might be more between them, but not now. Not after Dillon.

"I'm certain we can get you home tomorrow," Dillon said, returning from his survey of the creek.

"You probably want peace and quiet."

"I've enjoyed having you around. What? Are you accusing me of lying?"

"No, I'm certain integrity is your middle name."

Nothing less than the truth. She'd fallen for Dillon and leaving would break her. But he'd never request her to stay. She'd understood he intended to return to his soldier duties. Either way, she'd be alone.

"We have tonight." She added a wink even though the casual flirtation broke something inside her. "And I'm sure we'll meet at least once or twice before you leave."

"Count on it," Dillon said. "I'll ring Dad once we're finished for the day. I want to worm the alpacas before it gets dark."

"Can I help?"

"If you want."

About four hours later, Dillon bundled her into the shower for their second bathing session of the day.

His big hands cradled her face and held her still for his dominant kiss. Warm water poured over their heads, and her entire body tingled with sexual awareness. Dillon crowded her against the wall of the shower stall, the cold a sharp slap to her system. But then his big hands caressed her, his cock brushed her belly, and the discomfort faded. He grabbed a bar of soap and washed her with attention to detail. His fingers brushed and stroked, teasing and tantalizing. Her breasts rubbed against his chest, and she craved his hands and mouth at her nipples.

"More here," she instructed, lifting his hands to her breasts.

"I don't want to get too carried away. The condoms are in the bedroom."

"We'll go there," she said, urgency grabbing her. Ella tugged from his embrace and rinsed off the soap suds. "No point getting all excited and forgoing instant gratification."

After drying rapidly, a chuckling Dillon chased her to the bedroom. They fell on the bed in a tangle of limbs, urgency taking hold of them both. Dillon grabbed a condom and rolled it onto his shaft before planting himself in the center of the bed. With easy power, he lifted her over him, and she splayed her legs to straddle him.

"Take me," he said. "I want to enjoy the front view, see your tits bouncing as you take your pleasure."

In the grips of impatience, Ella guided his cock to her and sank down with a happy sigh. She rose and fell, finding a rhythm that suited her while falling into Dillon's pretty gaze. She took mental pictures of his handsome face, a vision to pull out at a later date when she found herself alone.

Not getting the stimulation she wanted, she added her finger to the mix and increased her pace. Ah, perfect. Her eyes drifted shut as she savored the emotions, the physical bliss frisking her body and mind. All the time, she rubbed her clit, striving for the finish post. One more stroke should do it. She timed her movements perfectly and fell into her orgasm, snatching greedily at every physical sensation.

"God, you're beautiful when you come."

Dillon flipped their bodies with easy strength and stroked into her with powerful thrusts. She gripped his shoulders and clung. His climax roared from him, his face tense, his cock flexing within her channel. Gradually, his big body relaxed, and he pressed a kiss to her jaw.

With her eyes closed, she smiled, happy and replete. "You didn't say if you liked your beard."

"You're hired," he said with a yawn.

But only short-term. A bitter-sweet moment.

"Are you hungry?"

"Not yet."

"Okay. Let's eat later. Right now, I'm too relaxed to move."

The soldier needed to catch up on his sleep. So did she. Ella yawned and allowed him to rearrange their bodies before she drifted off.

Ella woke abruptly in a dark room. A savage curse sounded right beside her ear, and instinctively, she backed away. Confused, she peered through the darkness, searching for anything. Then memories surged to her mind.

Dillon. She was staying at Dillon's place.

Restless legs shoved at her, and as she tried to avoid another kick, she toppled over the edge of the bed. She struck the floor with a thud, taking the brunt of the weight on her hip. Before she could pick herself up, a fist struck her jaw. Pain reverberated from the contact—short and sharp. She cried out, her shocked scream echoing through the bedroom.

"Don't move," a gritty voice snarled right next to her ear.

"Dillon?" she croaked. "Dillon, it's me. Ella. You're having a bad dream." At least she hoped he was because that would explain the fist to her face. "Dillon!"

The hands pinning her to the ground relaxed. Lifted. "Ella?" He sounded confused, a little out of it.

"Dillon, can you move so I can turn on the light?"

Crap, it hurt to talk, and she tasted blood. She needed to wake him before he decided she was the enemy and he hit her again.

6

A NIGHTMARE CHANGES DYNAMICS

DILLON BLINKED AT THE surge of light, his beleaguered mind ticking over the events. An enemy had sneaked into camp while he was sleeping. He'd attacked and Dillon had fought him off. Where the hell was his weapon? He'd never break the cardinal rule and leave his gun out of arm's reach.

"Dillon?"

A feminine voice. Cautious. Soft.

He tracked the direction, and his eyes widened. Fuck, he'd been dreaming. It hadn't been real.

"Dillon? Are you awake?"

"Yeah." He rubbed his hand over his face.

Ella came closer. Blood dribbled down her chin and her bottom lip was swelling. A bright red spot the size of a fist shone like a beacon and dread sliced through his belly, his chest. His limbs shook, and he couldn't have picked himself off the floor if he'd tried.

"Did…" He swallowed hard. "Did I do that?"

"You didn't mean to hurt me. You were dreaming. It took me a minute to understand." She trailed off with a wince.

"Fuck." Several other disgusting curses in foreign languages zapped through his brain as he stared at her, appalled. He'd never hit a woman in his life.

He eased closer, approaching her in increments. To his relief, she didn't back away or cower, but he wondered why. He'd bloody hit her. "Can I take a look?" He waited for her to give him the go-ahead.

"I'm okay."

He barely made contact, but she still flinched and guilt slid through him anew. "You've got a fat lip and your jaw is swelling. Let me get ice for you to put on that."

Dillon strode from his bedroom, calling himself all the names under the sun. This was a first for him. Beating a woman. Making her bleed. He yanked open the freezer compartment of his fridge, stared at the contents and chose a bag of peas. That should do the trick. Dillon wrapped a clean tea towel around the bag and took it to Ella.

"Hold this on your jaw. That should help reduce the swelling. Let me get a warm cloth for your lip and check the damage."

"Dillon, don't fuss."

"I hit you."

"You were dreaming. You didn't punch me on purpose."

"I'll get you pills for the pain. You should take those and

once I've cleaned your lip, try to go back to sleep."

She sent him a searching look before dipping her head in agreement.

Once he cleaned the blood off her face, he found the cut on her lip wasn't too bad. He settled Ella in bed then grabbed his jeans.

"Aren't you coming back to bed?"

"Not right now." He didn't trust himself. What if he struck her again? He might hospitalize her.

"I'm not scared of you."

He was slipping if she could read his thoughts this easily. Part of him ached to hold her, to tell her he'd never hit her again. His other tougher side told him to harden up. She said she was okay. Believe her and move on.

"Try to sleep. It's not long until morning."

He wandered out to the kitchen and his belly rumbled. They'd missed dinner. He checked the fridge, spied a dish of macaroni and cheese and set it in the microwave. While he waited for his meal to heat, he paced. Jitters made it impossible for him to sit still. His mind jumped around in tandem and a vision of himself striking Ella replayed over and over in his brain until he wanted to roar out his frustration.

Normally, he'd talk with his brother. A fellow SAS soldier, Josh understood what it was like to be away from home. He understood the dirty tactics of war and the way it played on a man. But Josh was in Afghanistan along with every other soldier Dillon might talk with about life and everything else. Talking helped. He knew it because he'd listened to others and taken his turn with the discussions.

Sharing with Josh had helped him decide he should take leave and get his head together.

The microwave pinged, but he ignored the summons. Instead, he tossed his sat-phone from hand to hand and considered the thought that had popped into his brain.

Nikolai.

While he hadn't liked the man at first and had ordered him away from Summer, things had changed. He'd grown to appreciate Nikolai Tarei and the way he was with Summer.

Decision made, he dialed.

"Yeah?" The gruff voice was thick with sleep. "Who is it?"

Dillon swallowed, his tongue thick with unspoken words. He cleared his throat and tried to decide where to start. Hana. The beginning.

"If this is a fuckin' prank call, I'm gonna reach down the phone and throttle you."

"It's Dillon. It's early but I need to talk and there's no one else."

"I'll go in the other room."

Dillon closed his eyes then opened the microwave to halt the infernal beeping. Macaroni and cheese wasn't appetizing anymore. He grabbed a beer instead and waited for Nikolai.

"Yeah."

"I have a guest sleeping over," Dillon said.

"A woman?" Nikolai sounded surprised.

"Ella."

"That was fast."

Dillon didn't get defensive since Nikolai's voice lacked judgment. "Hana. Our marriage was one of convenience so she could get out of Afghanistan. We were friends. Nothing more."

"Rumor said you stopped sleeping with other women once you married her."

Dillon huffed. His soldier mates gossiped worse than his mother and her cronies. "Once Hana and I married, it didn't seem right. I hated the idea of people whispering about her, so I didn't sleep around."

There was a moment of silence.

"She was a top woman," Nikolai said. "Everyone admired her work and professionalism."

"Yeah."

"What's the problem? No one could fault you for seeking feminine company."

"I had a dream and thought she was the enemy. I hit her. Gave her a bloody lip."

"Shit. She all right?"

"She says she is. Says she doesn't blame me."

"But you feel guilty."

"Wouldn't you?"

Nikolai hesitated. "Yeah, I'd worry about a repeat."

"A landslide blocked the road. I can't get Ella out until at least tomorrow because the creek is still flooded."

"You're sending her away? Summer would call that a cop-out."

Dillon grunted. "She'd be right. I've already lost one wife. I don't want to be responsible for someone else's safety. The guilt is bad enough now."

"The home invasion wasn't your fault. If you'd been there, the chances are you would've died too."

"My brain refuses to accept that, and now I've hurt Ella. Maybe I should leave and go elsewhere."

"You like this girl. I can tell."

"She makes me laugh."

"You?" Clear surprise sounded in his brother-in-law's voice.

"Fuck off. I smile."

"Rarely." Nikolai fell silent for an instant. "You could talk to a professional."

"No, it would go on my record."

"You're on leave. Find someone with a private practice."

"I'll consider it. The talk with you has helped."

"Another idea. I could get Summer to research useful books to help you through grief or PTSD. That sort of thing."

"She'd tell Mum and Dad."

"Not if I tell her it's for one of my trainees."

"You'd lie to your wife?"

"You could talk to Summer and ask her yourself. Remind her about the episode with the condoms and how you didn't rat her out to your parents."

Dillon sniggered, the memory of him and Josh walking in on Summer and Nikolai amusing him now. It hadn't at the time.

"Give me a few hours. I'll call you back if I decide to ask Summer for help."

"Make sure it's daylight when you call," Nikolai ordered.

"Sorry."

"Anytime, man. You could talk to your girl. Tell her what is going on in your head."

"It's too early. I'll make sure she gets back to her place tomorrow. Hell, today now. Give me a break."

"Some people might call that running away," Nikolai said, laughter in his voice.

"Fuck off. Talk to you later. Thanks, Nikolai."

Dillon hung up, lighter for having talked to his brother-in-law. It had helped him come to a decision. He'd give Ella space and take things from there.

He didn't bother going back to bed, but instead used the time to pay his bills and make a plan. Around eight, he looked in on Ella. She was still asleep. Dillon called his father to collect Ella and to ask about Hana's car again. He fed Rufus and let him run free while he pottered around with the alpacas. When he checked Ella the next time, she was in the shower.

Retreating again, Dillon made a pot of coffee and set the table. Ella arrived ten minutes later, and he winced on viewing her face.

"It's sore, but the pain is manageable," she said before he could comment.

"I'm sorry."

"It was an accident. It wasn't as if you meant to hit me."

"That doesn't make it any better. Cereal and toast okay for you this morning? We've run out of eggs." He poured a glass of water and handed it to her along with two tablets.

Ella swallowed the pills and took a seat at the kitchen table. "You didn't come back to bed."

"No, I was worried I might have another nightmare and hit you."

"You might have," she agreed. "But you can't go through life worrying about things that might or might not happen. That's not the way to live."

"I'm lucky I didn't hurt you worse." Dillon poured two mugs of coffee and added a smidge of milk to both. He set them on the table and returned to the counter to load bread into the toaster.

"Doesn't matter. End of discussion." She picked up her coffee and winced as she took a sip.

Remorse kicked him in the ribs at her clear discomfort. He'd put this right if he could, but there was no way to cure a bruised face.

"What are we doing today?"

"I've rung Dad, and he's driving to meet us. The weather is fine and we should be able to walk along the edge of the road and the pile of debris."

"You're getting rid of me?"

"No," Dillon snapped. "It's best if we get you home. The food supply won't last for much longer with two of us eating. On the plus side, we've made a dent in those casseroles."

Ella didn't laugh. "It would be good to have my own clothes again. When are we going?"

"We'll leave after breakfast." Well, that put him in his place. She hadn't argued about staying. Probably counting the minutes until their parting.

Unlike the rest of their meals, breakfast passed in silence, other than him asking if she wanted more coffee.

Ella didn't eat much and his ever-present guilt settled on his conscience. From the corner of his eye, he watched her try to eat a slice of toast and strawberry jam. Finally, she pushed her plate away.

"Finished?"

"Yes, thank you." Ella stood. "I'll help you with the dishes."

"Leave them. I'll do them later. I told Dad we'd be there around ten."

Ella nodded. "I'll get my handbag."

Dillon sighed as she disappeared. All their easy camaraderie had vanished, and he felt as if he was navigating a minefield. He plucked his keys off the hook in the kitchen. "I'll be outside when you're ready," he called down the passage.

"Be right there."

She emerged a few minutes later, carrying her handbag and a pile of clothes.

"I'll find a backpack for those. It will be easier when we walk out if you have the use of both hands."

The drive to the landslide took place in silence. Finally, Dillon switched on the radio, although the voices faded in and out and crackled, the hills blocking clear reception. He flipped it off.

"The creek level has dropped overnight," Ella said when she alighted from his vehicle.

Dillon nodded, agreeing with her assessment. "I'll carry your pack."

"I can do it."

"All right. Follow me and walk where I walk. I'm hoping

the ground isn't too unstable below the landslide area." After shoving his sat-phone securely in his pocket, he picked up a slasher instead of a spade and forged a path below the remnants of the road. He slashed through long grass and blackberry, the exertion causing sweat to slide down his spine.

Dillon paused. "How are you doing?"

"I'm fine." Mud splattered her sweatpants while the daylight highlighted her bruised jaw and swollen lip.

That guilt slipped to the foreground again. His father would comment for sure. Dillon forged a track closer to the creek. The ground was muddy and waterlogged underfoot and he slowed, stepping with caution on the sodden ground.

It was half an hour later before he got them back to the road. Both his parents were waiting.

"We were starting to worry," his mother said. "You've trimmed your beard. That's a huge improvement. You no longer resemble a wild mountain man."

"I didn't want to get too close to the landslide," Dillon said, ignoring the beard comment. If it wasn't for Ella, he'd still possess the out-of-control whiskers.

Ella stepped from behind him, and he spotted the instant his parents noticed her face. He worked at the impassive thing, which was bloody hard when culpability hounded him.

"Ella! Your face. You poor thing! Dillon said the landslide buried your car. How did you get out? Is that where you hurt your face?" His mother closed the distance between them and gave Ella a cautious hug. "You'll be pleased to get back to your own bed and routine."

"Yes," Ella said.

Most women of Dillon's acquaintance would've pointed the finger of blame at him and told the truth. Ella hadn't lied, but she let his parents assume she'd suffered the injury days ago instead of informing them their son was the culprit.

"I'd better get back," Dillon said. "I want to check on the rest of my fence since I didn't walk the entire boundary yesterday."

His mother frowned. "Are you sure you're okay for food, Dillon?"

"I'm right for a couple of days. By the weekend I'll need milk and a few staples."

"You should come home with us," she fretted.

"Leave the boy alone," his father said. "He's an adult, and he needs to watch over his animals. He'll let us know if he needs help."

"Thanks," Dillon said. "I'll call you. Ella, take care." With a wave, Dillon set off on the return journey to his vehicle.

The sound of his mother's chatter faded, replaced by the tweet of birds and the rush of the dirty water in the creek. As he neared his vehicle, half a dozen tiny green riflemen flitted from a tree. In the distance, a kereru, New Zealand's native wood pigeon cooed. The birds were plump and ungainly and made an audible *whop-whop* when they flew through the trees. Which reminded him of the helicopter landing at his neighbor's place.

He'd check his property boundaries and perhaps farther

beyond to appease his curiosity. His neighbor struck him as a rough-and-ready sort, and not the type to own a helicopter. The weather hadn't been right for spraying or a poison drop to combat the possum and rat problem. Yeah, his neighbor's business was none of his, but a jaunt to check things out would give him purpose. Something to do instead of worrying about Ella and how much he missed the woman.

How she'd wriggled under his skin in mere days, he was at a loss to explain. But she had, and he didn't want to remember her now or how he'd struck her. He desperately needed to keep his mind busy.

7

THE MYSTERIOUS DISCOVERY

MRS. WILLIAMS CHATTERED CONSTANTLY, which suited Ella fine. Her jaw throbbed and all she wanted to do was return to her cottage and relax in her own space.

"Would you like to come to dinner, dear?"

"Thanks for the offer, but I'm tired, and I have a project I was working on for my employer. I'm behind after getting trapped."

"Of course, dear. Another time. Do you like my son?"

"Marlene." Mr. Williams chided his wife. "Leave the poor girl alone. She's exhausted and I bet her jaw hurts. You're lucky you didn't get a black eye to go with your fat lip."

"Steven!" Mrs. Williams protested. "You'll have Ella conscious of her appearance."

"I saw myself in the mirror," Ella said.

Mrs. Williams peered at her in concern. "From what

Dillon said it sounds as if you were lucky not to get buried with your car."

Ella shuddered because she *had* been lucky. "Yes. Dillon was great. He's looking forward to returning to his work."

"Oh," Mrs. Williams said. "I was hoping I might persuade him to stay."

"Marlene, you promised not to pressure the boy."

Mrs. Williams sighed. "Why do my sons insist on the army? Why couldn't they be farmers like their father and grandfather? Then I wouldn't worry so much. I was hoping..." She glanced at her husband and trailed off. "I understand you're going out with Michael, dear."

"We were meant to go to dinner, but that wasn't possible with me trapped at Dillon's house."

"A pity," Mrs. Williams murmured.

It wasn't difficult to understand Mrs. Williams's angle. She'd hoped Ella might entice Dillon to stay. Unlikely, even though they'd enjoyed their days together. Friends with benefits. That was it, although things had become strained after Dillon had hit her. It had been an accident. She understood that.

Wrong time. Wrong place.

A pity because she enjoyed Dillon's company, but she'd move on and go out with Michael because she doubted Dillon would contact her now. He wore his regret and shame for striking her like a badge.

No, she'd place Dillon in her memories box and continue with her life. At least she might sleep now. She'd delivered Hana's message. Task completed. Job done.

"Ella?" Mrs. Williams's voice cut through her thoughts.

"Sorry. Did you say something?"

"Dillon suggested we lend you Hana's old car."

"Oh, that's unnecessary. I often bike to work since it's not far."

Mrs. Williams lifted her hand in a sign of dismissal. "Don't be silly, dear. The car is sitting in the garage gathering dust. We'll drop it off tomorrow."

"Thank you."

"You're welcome. Are you sure you don't need to go to the doctor? You're looking pale."

"I'm tired," Ella murmured. "That's all. It's been a long few days, and I never sleep well if I'm not in my bed."

"I can't believe Dillon made you sleep on the couch," Mrs. Williams retorted. "I taught him better than that."

"It was dry and safe. That was all that mattered." To Ella's relief, Mr. Williams pulled up in her driveway. "Thank you so much for collecting me. It would've been a long walk otherwise."

Ella pulled her keys out of her handbag, which was stuffed in the backpack Dillon had lent her.

"You're welcome." Mr. Williams's gaze drifted over her face and he frowned. "I'll leave the car keys on top of the right front tire, although I doubt anyone will try to steal it. It's not a pretty vehicle, but appearances are deceiving. It's got guts."

Ella slipped from the rear seat. "Thanks again." She waved as they drove off and released a slow breath. Dillon's mother was a cupid at heart, although Ella hadn't realized how determined she was to find her son a replacement spouse. She needed to back up a step. The poor man had only lost his wife six months ago.

She glanced at her watch, surprised to find it wasn't yet midday. It felt as if she'd been awake for hours. Her mind drifted to Dillon and regret filled her. She shrugged it off and padded the short passage to her bedroom.

A delightful interlude.

Yes, she'd call it that and move on with the rest of her life.

· ♥ · ♥ · ♥ · ♥ · ♥ ·

DILLON LEFT RUFUS AT home rather than walking him on a lead. For this mission, he required stealth. It wouldn't do for the neighbor to catch him skulking. A grunt of near humor escaped him. Must be more of his mother in him than he realized. This was the kind of thing she'd do when something piqued her curiosity.

He grunted again as he left his house, a pair of binoculars around his neck. He'd bet a crisp one-hundred-dollar note his mother had interrogated Ella during the drive back to her place.

Instead of heading straight for his boundary fence as he'd told himself he would, he took a roundabout route and watched the birds. Until Ella had mentioned it, he hadn't pondered the huge variety of native birds in his section of the bush. All he knew was they made a racket in the early morning. Hana had bird books somewhere. She'd written to him about them, saying she'd made the purchase because she wanted to learn about her new country.

God, she'd been happy and excited when he'd left the last time. Full of plans. She'd done many of the things on her list too, writing to tell him of the experiences and the new things she'd learned each week.

A pair of tui, the black birds with the tuft of white feathers on their throat, squabbled over territory while another tui somewhere to his right ran through his repertoire of guttural clicks and squawks. The tui were born mimics.

Overhead, a kaka, one of New Zealand's native parrots, squawked. When Dillon glanced upward, he caught a flash of orangey-red underwing as it flew over. The rest of the bird was an olive green.

Soon the birds ignored his silent, still presence. A fantail flitted to and fro, catching insects on the wing and maneuvering with its fanlike tail. The tui ceased their squabbling and settled to gather nectar from the treetop flowers.

Dillon used his binoculars to scan his vicinity and to get a closer view of the feeding tui. For a second, he didn't register the object, and he continued with his slow sweep of the trees. Then, he froze and retraced the visual path.

Son of a bitch.

That was a camera. He wouldn't have noticed it if he'd walked past but because he was stationery looking in the right direction, he'd spied it. What the devil was it doing here? And what was it for?

Puzzled, Dillon studied the angle of the lens. The camera was a light green and blended well with the treetops. No one watching the footage would spot him right now. The reasons for placing cameras on his property...

Nope, he couldn't decide on the rationale behind putting a camera there. If it was over the boundary fence on Pukaha Mt. Bruce property, he'd assume they were doing a tally of bird numbers or watching a particular nest for predators.

Did someone have a drug plot here in the bush? If that was the case, cameras made sense. Dillon did another sweep with his binoculars, this time searching for cameras. Then, he studied the ground in front of him. Yep, footprints. He hadn't noticed them earlier, hadn't been looking for them. He and Ella hadn't come this way yesterday, and he hadn't walked in this area for a few days.

The helicopter coming and going made more sense now if he factored in the assumption of drugs.

Dillon eyed the camera and slowly rose to his full height. A tui flew past and a faint light flickered. Not a flash, but more a sign that the camera was functioning. Ah, motion activated.

The tui hopped along a branch and flew away. The tiny green light flicked off. With his gaze on the camera, Dillon inched along the path. He wasn't certain of the range of the camera, and if someone walking caused it to click on, he didn't want his face recorded while gawking straight at the lens.

When nothing happened, he moved with more confidence. Chances were that he'd fail to spot all the cameras, so he paused now and then and peered through his binoculars. Twice, he pulled out his cell phone and took a photo.

If someone was growing drugs, why had the camera pointed at the trees? That made little sense. Of course, the storm might have blown the camera from its original position.

Even more curious now, Dillon continued to his boundary fence. He followed the fence line toward his neighbor's property, pausing frequently to scan the vicinity for further cameras and footprints.

He halted, frowning at the number of prints on the ground here. Crisp and defined, they didn't belong to him. He spotted another camera, this one pointing to the track he usually used when he checked the fences. Someone keeping a record of his whereabouts?

Dillon wasn't sure what to think.

He sank to the ground and waited, his mind busily calculating. If he had cameras on his land, what about the Mt. Bruce reserve? Dillon retreated. He'd enter the reserve at the far end of his property, rather than from this track where he'd spotted the camera.

But first, he needed better preparation. He sneaked past the camera, returned to his house and let out Rufus for a run while he grabbed a cup of tea and made a toasted sandwich.

Half an hour later, after eating and a change of clothes—something that blended better than his jeans and red-and-black Swanndri jacket—he put Rufus back in his run and set out armed with his binoculars and the camera Hana used to cart around with her everywhere. He'd charged it in case he wanted to take photos of whatever he discovered. If he missed a hidden camera and it filmed him, he wanted anyone viewing the footage to assume he was doing a spot of bird-watching.

Anticipation fueled him as he set out to the opposite end of his property. Once he entered the native bush, he dawdled, his binoculars tucked in his jacket pocket. Although he'd never bird-watched in his life—not the feathered variety at any rate—he settled in a likely spot and waited for activity.

Birds. People. Cameras. Anything out of the ordinary.

His interest had spiked after finding the camera, and now he wanted answers.

A fantail hopped along a branch above his head and took to the wing, its path erratic as it chased a bug. Dillon lifted his camera, aimed and took two photos. It didn't matter if his shots turned out blurry. Rather, he needed to look the part and blend.

When no other birds ventured near, he stood and headed deeper into the bush. Punga ferns with their silvery underside mixed in with towering rimu and matai trees. Beneath the canopy, smaller trees jostled for space. Dillon breathed in the green scents and the rich loamy aroma of the fallen leaves beneath his feet. Somewhere overhead, a bird sang in bell-like tones. He glanced up, trying to locate the songbird, but it blended well with the foliage.

In the distance, an engine of some sort fired to life, and he cocked his head, attempting to place the sound with the mental map he had of the area. The neighbor again. From memory, most of his property—at least the part bordering Dillon's land—was too steep for vehicles.

A chainsaw perhaps.

Dillon ghosted between the trees, moving silently with careful foot placement. It never hurt to hone his soldiering skills. He reached his boundary with the reserve twenty minutes later. The fence was post and wire. Nothing fancy, but enough to keep stock out of Pukaha Mt. Bruce land. The fence had been there for long enough that weeds—blackberry and gorse, flannel weed and other plants—grew on the cleared space. He'd bring a slasher with him next time.

He climbed over the fence. A group of massive kauri trees grew at the spot where he'd entered the reserve land. A bird shrieked, and he froze. A green parrot peered at him before continuing to crack the hard cones on the kauri trees. A second kaka flapped its wings, giving Dillon a glimpse of the red underside. He took a photo, grinning when the two parrots squabbled over food rights.

A small box sat in a tree, the color blending. When Dillon investigated, he noted the wooden steps cut into the tree trunk to enable someone to climb to retrieve the box. He set his camera and binoculars aside and made easy work of scaling the tree. When he went to open the box something rustled inside, and he started.

Hadn't expected that. With more caution, he climbed high enough to peer inside. A bird. Dillon frowned, not sure what to do. Was the reserve trapping birds? They'd called for local people to help with population counts, but they never captured the birds. He opened the trap and the bird huddled at the far end, terrified. He gave a soft tap and the bird scuttled away and literally fell to freedom. A kaka, he noted as the bird regained its sense and flew to a nearby branch.

Thoughtful, Dillon climbed back down the tree and reclaimed his binoculars and camera. He took a photo of the trap and continued with more caution.

Voices had him freezing in place. They were still a distance away. Could be people trekking through the forest, although from what Ella had told him, most visitors to the center stayed close and didn't attempt the more ambitious walks through the reserve.

Dillon edged away and took cover near the kauri trees. He ducked behind a mix of punga and other ferns and waited.

Two men appeared, each carrying a bag. One was a slight, skinny man wearing black jeans and a muddy black coat. The other man stood taller, around Dillon's height of six foot two. He had the look of a burly rugby player. Both were strangers to him.

The skinny dude planted his hands on his hips and stared at the trap. "Damn, I thought Jack said there was a bird in this one."

"We'll reset it," the other said. "It's your turn to climb."

The skinny man was a natural climber and scampered up the tree with the ease of a monkey. He pulled something out of his pocket—probably an enticement for a bird—and reset the trap. A few minutes later, the pair was on their way.

Dillon waited before following the men at a distance. They moved at speed, giving him the idea that they traveled a preset path. At each trap, they stopped. Most were empty and required resetting, but one held a bird. Its anxious squawks carried to him. The skinny man took away the entire trap and replaced it with another.

Wary of getting too close, Dillon missed most of what they said. Instead, he followed at a distance, making a mental note of the trap locations. When it was clear they'd finished their rounds, Dillon expected them to head down the hill. They didn't. They crossed over to his land and continued with their collection routine.

Right. These two men weren't from Pukaha Mt. Bruce then. Besides, he doubted the remit for the reserve included trapping birds in this manner.

Who the hell were these blokes?

Dillon didn't confront them. He needed more information. He needed to reconnoiter and plan. Once they finished on his land, they crossed to the reserve and disappeared deeper into the bush. He'd track them later, but first, he'd do some research.

8

HOME AGAIN TO FACE THE GOSSIP

ELLA RANG HER BOSS and confirmed she'd be back at work in the morning. Although her body ached and her head pounded, she didn't attempt to sleep now. If she did that, she'd never sleep tonight.

To ease the throb in her face, she took two more painkillers with a cup of mint tea, then attacked her laundry pile.

Disappointment sat like a sack of concrete on her shoulders, her weighty thoughts bearing down on her. She'd liked Dillon so much, and for him to turn away in the manner he had, irked her. She couldn't decide whether to heed his unsubtle warning and move on with her life or square her shoulders, lift her chin and wade into battle.

Dillon Williams was a decent man. A worthy one. While he was also grumpy and bossy and slotted into alpha man territory, his desirable traits far outweighed the bad. No wimpish lover for her. She'd hate a man who jumped at her every order. Her ideal lover was one who stood shoulder to shoulder with her, someone who embraced the word *team*. A man who held similar beliefs. A lover who argued with passion and fairness to sway her to his point of view.

A loud groan echoed through her miniscule laundry.

Dillon Williams was the one she craved.

A problem.

One: he intended to continue life as a soldier, which meant he jumped into dangerous situations.

Two: his emotions were all over the place, and she suspected he held a wheelbarrow full of guilt at Hana's death.

Three: he'd ordered her to move on and forget him.

Her phone rang, and pleased at the interruption, she hustled to the kitchen where she'd left her cell phone to answer the call.

"Hey, Ella," her friend Suzie warbled down the line. "You're home. Gossip mill says you got yourself stranded with Dillon Williams. Is that true?"

Ella laughed. "Depends on what you've gleaned from the rumors."

"Why don't we meet for a coffee in town? You can give me the lowdown, and I'll give you details of the rumors," Suzie said.

"You'll have to drive. My car is buried under the landslide."

"Oh my god! That part is true? Are you okay? I was certain the story had grown and taken on a life of its own."

Ella waited until her friend's verbal batteries ran down

before she said, "I have a fat lip and a sore jaw to prove it."

"Oh, Ella. It sounds as if it could've been much worse." Sympathy coated her friend's words. "Do you prefer to stay at home?"

Ella considered and decided she'd set the story straight with Suzie and her other acquaintances. And, she'd get out of the house and away from her busy thoughts. Two birds. One stone. "Can you pick me up?"

"Sure."

"Give me half an hour before you leave home. That will give me a chance to have a shower and change my clothes. I haven't been home for long."

By the time Suzie arrived, Ella had showered and applied makeup to cover the worst of the damage on her face. Her top lip appeared fuller than normal, but apart from that, she didn't look much different.

"Your face isn't too bad. I thought it would be worse." Suzie had confined her black hair in a braid and donned light makeup to enhance the light brown skin from her part-Maori heritage.

Ella smiled with caution and barely flinched at the pull of facial muscles. "Makeup."

"Are you ready to go?"

"Sure." Ella followed Suzie out to her car.

"It sounds as if you had a lucky escape. How are you going to get around without a car? Have you rung the insurance company?"

"Not yet. I'll do that after our coffee."

Suzie filled the five-minute drive into Eketahuna with her normal scatter-gun chatter. "Jenny broke up with

Daniel. They've been going out together *forever*! No one has the deets and neither of them is talking."

"That's a shame. Jenny told me they were getting engaged soon." Ella was glad the spotlight had left her for the moment. She didn't like lying to her friend, but if she shared the events with Suzie, the story would race through Eketahuna before Ella reached her cottage again.

Their favorite café was still busy with the lunch time tail of customers. A flyer in the café window snared her attention.

"Oh, look. It must be kismet. They're doing spinning classes. I promised myself I'd learn since I have the spinning wheel."

Suzie snapped a photo to record the details. "They have a knitting class too. We can drive to the classes together."

"Deal," Ella said as she followed Suzie inside.

The chatter died a fraction after they entered, and Ella's spine stiffened. This was the part about small country town living that drove her batty. Everyone liked to share their opinion about *everything*.

"Do you want your usual, Suzie? It's my turn to buy."

"I'm in a hot chocolate mood today. Plead for extra marshmallows. I'll grab a table."

A group of four women stood as Ella walked past. Their lined faces shone with nosy curiosity.

"Ella." The elderly lady's gnarled right hand curled around the head of a black walking stick and she knocked it twice on the tiled floor as if demanding attention. "Rumor says you stayed at Dillon Williams's place. Are you going out with him now?"

"What? No! He owns alpacas, and I wanted to buy fleece from him. A landslide blocked the road when I was leaving and almost covered my car."

"A slip? Right on your car? Oh, my," another of the elderly ladies commented, this one tall and rail thin in her straight burgundy skirt, pink twinset, and pearls. She patted her flat chest in horror.

"Someone told me your car was buried," a third woman declared. She wore muffin crumbs on her ample bosom and grasped the handlebars of a walker to keep herself upright.

"Oh, it was," Ella said, thrilled that not one of them had noticed her face. "I climbed out and walked back to Dillon's place since it was obvious I wouldn't be driving anywhere. When we checked the next day, more of the hill had slipped away and buried my little car."

"And you stayed with Dillon Williams all that time?" the fourth woman asked, her eyes glinting behind her horn-rimmed spectacles. Her flaring nostrils and close attention brought to mind a drug-sniffer dog.

"Yes, I slept on the couch and have a sore neck to prove it. I'm glad I'll be in my bed tonight."

"Of course, dear." The lady with the walker gave her a hard stare but Ella never flinched.

"I must order our coffee," Ella said. "It was nice chatting to you." She stood back to allow the quartet to pass before she approached the counter.

The young employee—a school leaver the previous year—plied her own nosy questions and giggled at the mention of Dillon. "Now getting trapped with Josh, his younger brother, would work for me," she said with another high-pitch giggle and a hair twirl.

After Ella repeated her story and placed her order, she wove through the tables and sank onto a seat at the table Suzie had chosen.

Suzie glanced around the café and leaned closer. "Now tell me what really happened."

"I told them the truth. The landslide almost buried me. I walked back to Dillon's house and slept on his couch."

"What about your reason for visiting him in the first place?"

"I have my mother's spinning wheel. You know I've wanted to try my hand at spinning for ages, and I need raw materials. Dillon has alpacas, therefore it's a match made in heaven."

Suzie wrinkled her nose. "Not exactly what I meant. Besides, you can't spin yet."

"I've learned enough! Honestly, there is nothing of note to tell you." Ella leaned back when the waitress arrived with their hot drinks and two cheese scones. "The worst part is getting hold of that fleece now that the road is blocked. I'll have to find another source. I'm sold on the idea of alpaca rather than sheep's wool. Washing the wool to get rid of the oil is a pain." There! She hadn't committed too many large lies.

"Spinning is difficult. My sister tried it and her yarn was full of lumps."

"I'm sure mine will be too, but they say practice makes perfect for a reason."

"Is he still cute? He and his younger brother used to stop

traffic. Gina Attcastle ran into the back of Mrs. Heritage's car because she was gawking at their backsides. That would be Dillon's and Josh's rear ends, in case I wasn't clear."

"Well, his body is all muscle and he has an exceptional arse—from what I saw, but he has a huge black bushy beard. You remember that television reality show about mountain men and ducks?" Ella shook her head at Suzie's vacant stare. "Never mind. Imagine Santa Claus with a bushy black beard and you'll start to get the picture."

Again, her lies weren't too big, and the last thing she needed was for Suzie to decide she was hiding something.

"To be honest, I'm glad to be home. My only regret is the alpaca fleece. I might have to resort to practicing on sheep's wool, despite my reservations."

· ♥ · ♥ · ♥ · ♥ · ♥ ·

DILLON HAD PLENTY TO keep him busy, but Ella kept intruding. She tiptoed into his mind during his shower and never left, despite his efforts to shove her out. When that failed, he dragged thoughts of native birds, cameras, and helicopters to the forefront and pushed Ella back. That only worked for ten minutes.

He missed her.

A scowl dug into his cheeks. He had no idea how but the woman had wriggled under his skin like a tropical burrowing insect.

Dillon shunted his focus back to the native birds. He needed a research whiz. Pleased he'd thought of his sister, he started to dial then stopped. Summer might tell their mother. He hesitated until a plan skittered to mind. Blackmail. Summer had kept details of her adventure in Auckland to herself, and he and Josh hadn't blabbed. Yet. Their mother had stressed enough about her youngest living in the big city of Auckland. If she learned she'd been right to worry, Summer would receive many, many lectures.

Yeah, if he played the blackmail card with his sister he should be safe from parental lectures and concern.

He redialed Nikolai's number.

"It's Dillon," he said when Nikolai answered.

"This is getting to be a habit," Nikolai said. "You okay?"

"Better. Ella went home this morning. I'm ringing about something else. I need Summer's help, but I wanted to run it past you first."

"All right."

"I've stumbled on something here. How much of a demand is there for our native birds on the black market? Could Summer research that for me? Without mentioning anything to my parents? I hate to worry them."

"You suspect that's happening?"

"Signs point that way, but I need to check more closely on my neighbor."

Nikolai remained silent for a beat. "Is he trapped behind the landslide too?"

"Yep. Ah! You think a neighborly visit might work or at least give me an in."

"That's what I'd do. Visit and see if my spidey senses sing."

Not a bad idea. But a visit might also stir the pot and raise warning signals. Something to consider.

"What made you suspicious?"

"The appearance of a helicopter. It wasn't one belonging to the local outfit that does spraying. No logos on the side, but a private bird. I can't figure out why it would land at my neighbor's place. That made me curious. I discovered a camera on my land. When I poked around, I found two bird traps in the trees and released a captured bird. Then, two workers came along, checking the traps. I intend to reconnoiter tonight and investigate."

"Do you have a guess for how many workers your neighbor employs?"

"No, the neighbor's farm is bigger than mine. I've only met him once, and he's as rough as guts. He didn't give me the impression of a successful farmer."

"You suspect he's found a lucrative way to increase his income."

"Possibly. The things I've discovered point that way, but I might be wrong."

"You Williamses have a nose for trouble."

Dillon laughed. "Can Summer research for me? I want estimates of how much our rarer native birds might fetch on the black market. I've noted signs of kiwi on my property. And because my land borders Pukaha Mt. Bruce, populations of the rarer birds spill over to the neighboring bush."

"I'll speak to Summer," Nikolai said.

"And you'll mention she shouldn't tell our parents, especially Mum. Tell her I'll spill about her adventures in

Auckland if she blabs."

"Ah, sibling blackmail. Makes me glad I was a lone child. Text me when you're leaving and when you return," Nikolai said. "If you need help, it won't take me long to fly to Palmerston North. Louie and Jake might enjoy an outing too."

"Thanks. I'll keep that in mind."

"Knowing Summer, she'll have the info for you by the morning. The kid is keeping us awake."

Dillon grinned. "Give my nephew a hug."

"Will do. Keep me posted."

Dillon hung up and decided he was hungry. He opened the fridge, peered at the dwindling contents and scowled.

He heated yet another stew, and his thoughts slipped to Ella. Again.

"You could always ring her, check on her."

He frowned. Why the devil did the voice in his head sound like Hana?

Dillon rifled through the cupboard and found a sachet of quick-cook rice. Once he'd heated that, he tipped it into a bowl and added the stew.

The entire time, the tiny voice yammered. *"Ring Ella. You should call. Find out how she is tonight. You hit her."*

He shoveled the stew and rice into his mouth, no longer hungry but eating because he required fuel to function.

"Ring, Ella."

"All right," he snapped. "I'll do it. Just let me eat my dinner first."

To his relief, the tiny voice fell silent.

Once he finished dinner, he washed the few dishes

and cleared the surfaces. The voice started again, and he suspected it wasn't in his head.

"Hana," he barked.

The voice fell silent.

Dillon swiped a cloth across his counter surfaces. Then, he grabbed his sat-phone and stomped to the lounge. He switched on the television and channel surfed until he came across a crime show he enjoyed.

The voice whispered, and this time, an echo reached him. He did not believe in ghosts. He. Did. Not.

Yet he couldn't deny the spooky chatter. He'd dismissed Ella's claims and sent her on her way. But they weren't both crazy.

He clenched his sat-phone and stared in the direction of the last whisper. "I'm ringing Ella to make sure she's okay, not because you're nagging me."

He dialed, his stomach churning with unaccountable nerves. The phone rang several times. Five. Six. Just as he was about to hang up and call himself stupid, she answered.

"Hello?"

"Ella, it's me. Dillon."

"Dillon, you've been in my thoughts."

No pretense. Most women of his acquaintance would've pretended they were busy. Too busy to bring him to mind.

"How are you?" He hesitated and decided he could be equally honest. "How is your face? Are you still in pain?"

"A little. The painkillers help. I miss you. I don't know how that happened. We spent three days together and I feel as if it has been years."

"Did I wake you?"

"I couldn't sleep. Ah...your wife..." She trailed off with an audible swallow. "You don't believe me. But there is this insistent voice and once it starts, it doesn't stop."

"I've heard her," Dillon said. "At first I thought the voice was in my head. It's not. It sounds like Hana."

"Your mother is a matchmaker."

Dillon groaned. "I'm sorry."

"I let nothing slip. She thinks I slept on the couch. Suzie, one of my friends, and I had coffee in town. Everyone wanted the details."

"I'm sorry. For everything." For a second, he debated telling her about the birds, then he changed his mind. If his neighbor had big money at stake, things might get dangerous when he poked around.

"I meant to purchase alpaca fleece from you. That's what I've been telling everyone. That I drove to your place to collect fleece because I wanted to start spinning."

"I'll make sure I keep our stories straight."

"Dillon, I told myself to ignore you and move on with my life. But... I want to keep seeing you. Um...I want you in my bed."

He found himself smiling. "So it wouldn't upset you if I arrived at your backdoor one night."

"You can visit me any time. You don't have to sneak."

"I do in order to keep my mother oblivious."

"Okay then." Ella sounded happier than when she'd first answered his call.

"What about Michael? If there is a chance of a

110

relationship with him, I'll stay away."

"I...no. I've spoken to Michael and told him I'm not ready for another relationship."

"And if he finds out about us?"

"I don't blab. I never have and I'm not about to start."

He grinned at the pert note in her voice. "Do you have plans for tomorrow night?"

"I have a book club meeting. Not that I've finished the book yet. I'm finding it hard-going."

"Not another book about men's backsides?"

"No, it's about this man in Russia. I land firmly in the genre fiction camp. Mainly romance, and I enjoy a sprinkling of non-fiction. What about you?"

"When I read, I enjoy something light and humorous. Mysteries are good. I live through enough drama and gunfights without reading about them. Westerns are okay. I don't mind those."

"Do you listen to music or audio books?"

"I hadn't considered audio books. That might be a change."

They chatted for a bit longer before they hung up.

"Okay, Hana, if you're not a figment of my imagination. I've called her but there's no chance of a future. I'm a career soldier. It's what I do."

But he hadn't always been that way. He and Hana had discussed his retirement. They'd both wanted a simpler life. Eventually.

Things had changed after Hana's death. Her murder had rocked him. Made him reassess.

When he'd first come home, he'd harbored a vague idea

about investigating her murder. He'd visited the local cops, and they'd told him what they could.

Whoever had murdered Hana had struck her head. They hadn't raped her but she'd worn defensive wounds. No matches for DNA found on the scene. Money and her mother's jewelry had disappeared, along with a laptop, a tablet, and other electrical gear.

Bottom line—the police were at a loss.

No other aggregated robberies or other home invasions reported in the area, apart from the one closer to Masterton.

The trail had gone cold.

But what if Hana had come across the same things he'd discovered since being at home?

She'd loved the birds and had told him she was making a list of the species she'd spotted.

Something to consider.

A yawn had him deciding to head to bed. Rather than blundering around in the dark, he'd set the alarm for dawn. He tapped out a quick message to Nikolai, informing him of his change of plans then hit the sack.

Dillon woke before the alarm buzzed. A tui called from a tree outside, determined to rouse him before full light. A groan escaped. Another night of restless sleep, except this time Ella had filled his dreams. Sex dreams. Damn, he hadn't had one of those for a while.

Again, he dressed in clothing to blend. He even considered green paint for his face, but if someone caught him, he hated to invite extra questions. With camera and binoculars in hand, he set off at a brisk pace.

He headed straight for his boundary and scaled the fence, slipping into the Mt. Bruce property. It was light enough now for him to watch his foot placement. Birds sang and squawked, greeting the day. The melodic song of the bellbird dominated the dawn chorus, giving Dillon an idea of how it must've been before man decimated the New Zealand forest.

He spotted another camera, which meant backtracking and approaching from a different direction. Since he wasn't on his land, he wanted to make sure the camera owner didn't spot him. He also saw several bird traps, two with captive birds. He released them and took pleasure in the act.

Last night, he'd studied the plans for his land and he'd confirmed the boundaries of his neighbor's property. He hit the first fence and scaled it. Once he trespassed on his neighbor's land, he noticed a higher concentration of traps. A couple held birds, but he left these in the interest of time. He wanted to poke around more before he left.

He scaled a hill and paused at the summit. From where he stood, he had a view of the neighbor's house and farm buildings, which were nestled in a protected valley. Cattle grazed in several paddocks, but not the numbers he would've assumed given the man's acreage.

With a practiced eye, he analyzed the area around the farm buildings, the places where he could take cover if necessary, and the most likely buildings to house birds. No helicopter in evidence. After his visual examination of the scene, he scanned with binoculars in case he'd missed anything. Lastly, he took photos of the layout to study later at home.

After a final careful scan for people, he started his descent toward his neighbor's home.

If someone caught him, he hoped to talk his way out of the situation. Humor flashed through him and had him grinning. Difficult to explain the camo clothes. However, from his observations, avid birdwatchers could be eccentric. He often acted a part during their missions. Playing the part of an odd-ball birdwatcher—easier than a Sunday stroll.

Dillon darted from trees to dips in the land's contour. Halfway down the hill, he stopped to reconnoiter. Still quiet. Now that he was closer, he moved steadily rather than running. If anyone was watching his descent, he wanted them to think birdwatcher. Something told him birdwatchers seldom ran through the bush since scaring every bird in the vicinity defeated the purpose.

Steadily, he continued toward his goal. A flashy utility truck sat in front of a sagging house. The lawn around the house had grown to knee-height. Dillon approached the first of the outbuildings. After a glance over his shoulder, he tried the door. It opened with a loud, protesting creak, and he froze. A beat later, he stepped inside. A quick glance told him it contained farm equipment.

His watch warned of the rapidly advancing hour. He poked his head from the shed, and finding the way clear, he slid along the side of the corrugated iron building without bothering to close the door.

Voices had him freezing at the corner of the shed. Had

they discovered his presence or was it starting time for the workers?

Two men. Dillon risked a glance around the corner and spotted the two men standing outside the largest of the four outbuildings. He watched one punch in a code to open the door. Suspicions raised, Dillon waited for both men to disappear inside.

He was about to risk moving closer when one man exited and strode toward the farmhouse.

Damn, he needed to check inside that shed, but it wouldn't be today.

Dillon retreated, none of his curiosity appeased. Instead, more questions filled him while his gut screamed his initial suspicions were right.

His neighbor might have cattle on his property, but they weren't his main source of income.

· ♥ · ♥ · ♥ · ♥ · ♥ ·

ELLA TOSSED AND TURNED for the entire night and was almost relieved when the alarm announced it was time for her to start her day.

She crawled out of bed and fell into the shower, standing under the warm water for a long time. Not that it did much to counteract her dozy state. She wiped the mirror, taking pleasure in wiping away her name, shakily written in the condensation. Her jaw ached, the bruise more noticeable this morning. Her entire body cried for sleep, and she wasn't sure how she'd get through the day.

In the kitchen, she made a pot of tea and tried to ignore

the whispers.

"Ella. Ella. Ella."

The cup and saucer she'd placed on the kitchen counter rattled. Milk splattered onto the counter.

Ella, who was peering in her fridge, whirled at the sudden racket. She turned in time to witness the cup tipping off the saucer. It skidded across the countertop and dropped over the edge. The china struck the floor tiles and smashed into three big pieces and myriad shards.

Ella stared at the remnants of the cup—her favorite one. Her hands tightened to fists, and she sucked in an audible breath, striving for calm when the instinct to wail like an Irish banshee fought for precedence.

On the counter, the saucer rattled and shook. It scooted toward the edge, and Ella lost it.

"Why won't you go? I did what you asked. Just leave me alone!"

"Ella. Ella. Ella."

The small hairs at the back of Ella's nape lifted. Tears pricked in her eyes, fueled by frustration and exhaustion.

"I can't butt into Dillon's life. He already thinks I'm a kook. I have to go to work." She scowled at the saucer that teetered half off the counter. Then, she shifted her attention to the cup lying on her floor. "Maybe you could use your ghostly powers to pick that up for me."

She stomped back to her bedroom to pull on her uniform. After shoving her purse and a coat in Dillon's day pack, she left her cottage.

Since the promised car hadn't arrived yet, she rode her bike. The ride to Pukaha Mt. Bruce was normally enjoyable, but today with exhaustion trailing her like a family pet, she wasn't in the mood for fresh air and chirpiness.

Ella shouted a rude word at the driver of a Mitsubishi and punctuated it with an appropriate gesture. Moron! If she'd pulled any farther off the road, she'd be in the ditch.

It was with relief she reached her workplace. At least the ghost had never bothered her here. A glance at her watch told her she had time for coffee before she started her workday. She left her bike in the employee carpark and forced her legs to take her to the entrance.

"Good morning," she said to Joy.

"Ella. Oh! Your face. You look terrible." Joy rushed around the shop counter where they sold souvenirs and visitors paid the entrance fee to the reserve. "Should you be back at work?"

"I'll be fine after a coffee," Ella said, forcing a smile even though that made her face hurt. Her makeup hadn't covered the deeper bruising this morning. "Is Marie here? I'm not sure where I'm meant to work today."

"You're down to do the eel feeding, and the staff on the kiwi house need help. Someone has to watch Kura and Boy while they're getting acquainted, and you're familiar with the routine."

"All right. I'll grab a coffee from the café before I check in with Marie."

Five minutes later, coffee in hand, Ella knocked on Marie's door.

"Come in."

Ella walked into Marie's office. "Hi, Mar—"

Marie's eyes widened behind her glasses, and she shot to her feet. "Ella, you look dreadful. I didn't realize your injuries were this serious."

"Thanks," Ella said drily.

"No offense meant. Why don't you take the rest of the week off? Return to work on Monday. That will give you five days to recuperate."

Ella sank onto the chair that sat in front of Marie's desk. "Are you sure?"

"Yes, of course. You look as if you might collapse."

Ella nodded and grimaced. Marie wasn't wrong. "Okay, thanks." She stood. "I'll be here on Monday."

The cycle ride back to her cottage held a slight incline, and by the time, she turned into her driveway, every muscle in her body protested. Her head thumped in tandem, and she almost fell flat on her face while trying to dismount her cycle.

"Ella. Ella. Ella."

The whispers started the instant she unlocked her front door and staggered inside. Ella ignored them although this proved difficult with cold prickling at her nape. After a hot shower to ease her muscles, she changed into casual clothes and her favorite lilac jersey for a mood boost.

With a heavy sigh, she walked to the kitchen and collected her broom and dustpan. Not only had the ghost not cleared the pieces, but the saucer had joined her cup on the floor. Crockery rattled and clinked as she directed it with her broom. Finally, Ella straightened with a groan.

"Ella. Ella. Ella."

A car sounded in the driveway. She peeked out the

kitchen window and spotted Dillon's mother.

"Oh, you're here," Mrs. Williams said when Ella stepped outside. "Oh, dear. You look dreadful."

Ella attempted to straighten her posture. Her teeth clenched as she fought a groan. "So everyone has been telling me. Marie gave me a few days off."

Mr. Williams parked behind his wife's vehicle.

"The tank is half full." Mrs. Williams handed over the keys.

"Thank you. I rang my insurance company yesterday afternoon. They want a police report and photos." Which meant returning to the scene of the crime. She wished she'd taken a photo earlier.

"Rather you than me," Mr. William said. "I hate dealing with insurance companies."

"Ella. Ella. Ella."

"Did you hear something?" Mrs. Williams asked.

"No," Ella lied, her hands clenching at her sides. If she could get her hands on that ghost...

"But I'm sure..." Mrs. Williams's cell phone peeled out a tuneful military march. "Oh, that's my daughter's ringtone." She pulled her phone from her handbag and stabbed a button. "Summer. I wasn't expecting a call." She listened for an instant. "Oh, that's wonderful news. Tomorrow? What? When? Your father and I will come and get you. Oh. Okay. We'll expect you early afternoon. I can't wait to cuddle our grandson. I bet he's grown."

She returned her phone to her purse and beamed.

"I take it Summer is coming home," Mr. Williams said.

"Yes, Nikolai has a few days off work, and they decided

they'd visit. We'd better go. I'll need to run to the supermarket and give the spare room a spring clean."

"Thank you for dropping off the car," Ella said.

Mr. Williams patted her on the shoulder. "You keep the car for as long as you need it."

"Ella. Ella. Ella."

Mr. Williams frowned while Ella kept her face impassive, pretending innocence.

"Steven, we'd better go. I need to hustle before Summer and Nikolai arrive," Mrs. Williams said.

"Thanks again." Ella waved good bye. "Well, that was fun. Both Mr. and Mrs. Williams overheard your whispering. If I'd known I was getting a ghost with the cottage, I might have picked the farm house on the other side of town."

Ella limped back inside, wondering how to fill the hours. If she slept now, she'd spend most of the night awake again.

Maybe she'd get out her camera and drive to the landslide. She'd take her photos to add to her insurance claim then head off to the police station. No, she'd curl up and watch the taped episodes of the *Brokenwood Mysteries*. In her opinion, the small-town New Zealand show was on a par with *Midsomer Murders*.

Later that night, Ella stared into her pantry with disinterest. Soup. Simple and quick. She reached for a can of chicken soup as someone knocked at the door.

One of her friends, no doubt, to check on her. She yanked open the door.

"Don't you have a security chain?" Dillon scowled. "I could be anyone."

120

"If you're going to be snarly, go away. I'm not in the mood to deal with cantankerous men."

The man stared at her, then chuckled.

Enough. Ella let out a snarl of her own and shoved the door. He stopped her by putting his boot in the doorway.

"Aren't you going to let me inside? Crap, your face looks bad."

"So everyone keeps telling me." Ella folded her arms and tried to hide her wince. Even blinking hurt today. "What do you want? I'd decided on a quiet evening. I'm not even going to the book club meeting."

He shut the door with a solid click and turned the key.

Ella's eyes widened. "You've locked yourself inside with me, why?"

"We're doing the friends with benefits thing tonight."

Ella sniffed. "I'm tired. Every part of my body aches. Go away."

"Fair enough. I can deal with that. What are we having for dinner?" Dillon lifted his head and sniffed. "Not one delicious aroma."

"I was having soup. I suppose I can make pasta too." The words emerged grudging with that side of temper still simmering. Not helped by his arrogance.

"Works for me," Dillon said. "Give me my orders."

Ella sighed. "If you won't leave, you can chop an onion."

"I'm a champion onion chopper."

Ella's mouth stretched until her jaw pulled. "Someone thinks highly of himself."

"Confidence is key in most things. I'll need to wash my hands. Point me toward the bathroom."

"Through there." She pointed. "It's the first door on the left."

Dillon disappeared, his footsteps silent. A soldier thing. *Obviously*. Ella pulled the ingredients they'd need out of the cupboard and found her lips curving just a little. Her apathy had lifted with his arrival. She'd told Suzie she wanted to be alone when her friend had checked on her, but Dillon's presence was welcome.

"Ella. Ella. Dillon."

"That's a new one," she muttered as she placed an onion and two segments of garlic on the counter. She pulled out a knife and a chopping board for Dillon's use.

"How was work today?" Dillon asked on his return.

"Some idiot driver tried to run me off the road during the bike ride there. And once I got to work, everyone said my appearance scared them, and my boss sent me home. I'm allowed to go back to work on Monday. What did you do?"

"I went bird-watching early this morning."

"Pardon?"

"I think my neighbor is illegally trapping native birds. I suspect he's selling them on the black market."

Ella gaped at Dillon. "Are you sure?"

"No, I'm not certain. My plan is to confirm my suspicions, then I'll report him to the cops and the Department of Conservation."

"There are kiwi, kokako and other rare birds living in the area," Ella said, her mind racing. Shock. Horror that anyone would consider this theft. The birds were a national treasure.

"Yes, I imagine that's why they've started the business here." Dillon peeled and chopped the onion with military precision while Ella dealt with the portobello mushrooms.

She heated oil in a frying pan and added the onion and garlic, shunting it around the sizzling surface with a bright blue spoon. "I understand your sister is coming home for a visit. Your mother is excited."

"You saw my parents?"

"They delivered the car for me. Thanks, by the way."

He shrugged. "No problem. Nikolai and Summer decided I needed help to investigate, and Summer figured she'd keep Mum busy while Nikolai and I poked around."

"Excellent strategy." Ella's lips quirked in a half-grin.

"Summer is acting smug after thinking of it," Dillon said with a big-brother eye roll.

"Do you have a plan?"

"I need to get into the shed where they're keeping the captured birds. Or rather, where I suspect they're holding them. I came across several traps yesterday. I released the birds."

"That must've irked the people involved."

"Yeah. They almost caught me."

Ella stared. "Are they dangerous?"

"They didn't appear to carry weapons, but they might have concealed them."

"Ella. Ella. Ella."

"Did you hear that?" Dillon's voice was sharp.

"I try to ignore her, although that didn't work last night. I didn't get much sleep."

His brows rose halfway to his hairline. "Hana?"

123

"Dillon."

Dillon's gaze shot to Ella. His head jerked in a tiny shake of denial while his focus hinted at a soldier mind working at warp-speed.

"What?"

"That wasn't you."

Ella crossed her arms. "Did you see my mouth moving?"

"No, but I doubted you."

"Fine. You're sorry for treating me like an imbecile. All I wanted was for it to stop. If you can make her stop, you'll be my hero. I hardly slept last night, and it wasn't just my bumps and bruises."

"How am I going to stop her haunting you?"

"If I knew, I would've done it already," Ella snapped and applied her frustration to swishing the onion and garlic around her pan. "It's not as if there's a guide book for this kind of thing. She has been extra chatty since I returned. Between the dreams and the chatter... Let's just say Hana doesn't seem to think sleep is a priority for me."

"No." Dillon's lips twitched.

"It's not funny. You try going without sleep for days. That's why I finally gave in and visited you."

"And I thought you were after my body." Dillon's grin widened, and it echoed in the shine of his eyes. "Hana, what do you want?"

Ella held her breath and listened. Nothing happened. *Of course.*

Dillon shrugged. "Guess I'm not having any better luck than you. What should I do next?"

"Open the can of soup for me, please. There's a small

pot in the bottom cupboard." She gestured. "Can opener in the drawer there."

Ella added the mushrooms to the pan, then grabbed the jar of penne pasta from the pantry. "Do you eat seafood? Prawns?"

"I eat most things."

"Great." That made things easy. She filled a saucepan with hot water and put it on to boil, happier now that Dillon was here. Her mind wanted to analyze this fact, but she forced herself to divert to other things. "I have a question. Why don't you go to the cops, tell them what you suspect and leave the entire mess to them?"

Dillon heaved out a sigh. "That's what a sensible man would do. I don't know. It burns me that a neighbor, hell, a fellow New Zealander, might do this. Hana loved her new country. The green of our land after the barrenness of the desert where she lived and worked. The birds fascinated her, the alpacas. The freedom. Part of me wants to investigate and do this for Hana. I couldn't be here for her before, but perhaps this can be my shout out for her. Something she'd approve of."

The water in the pot came to a rolling boil, and Ella dumped in the pasta. "In a weird way that makes sense. Hana was lucky to have you."

Ella paused, wondering if her frustrating ghost might have a comment. But no. Silence reigned.

"Hana lived in this cottage for a while before we got married." He frowned and appeared to drift into the past.

Ella left him to his thoughts and poured the soup into two bowls.

"I'll get those," he said.

"Thanks." Ella checked the timer for the pasta then walked into the pantry to search out a container of home-made garlic croutons she'd made the previous week. Ah! She seized them and joined Dillon in her dining room. "Croutons?"

"Sure."

Ella ate alone several nights a week and never minded her own company since she balanced this out with social weekends. In her mind, this dinner with Dillon felt like a date, and the acknowledgement brought a frown.

"This is slipping into date territory," she blurted.

"Excellent." Dillon applied himself to his soup.

Ella scowled at her bowl, tension creeping into her hand until she strangled her spoon. In the kitchen, the timer summoned her with a pesky *beep-beep-beep*.

"Saved by the bell," Dillon quipped.

"Did Hana find you irritating?"

"Of course. We were friends and had good and bad days." Dillon never hesitated. "None of us is perfect."

"Hmmm." Ella stood to sort out her pasta.

After dinner, they sat on the couch and watched an action movie. The hero amused Dillon, who criticized his actions and use of weapons during the tension-filled scenes. And he scoffed at the romantic scenes, which took place while the villains were hot on their trail.

Conscious of both the ghost and Dillon's arm thrown around her shoulder, Ella had difficulty concentrating, although her non-committal murmurs satisfied Dillon. When the closing credits rolled across the screen, she voiced her questions.

"What exactly are you going to do next?"

"My brother-in-law is a trainer for the Army. He will help me formulate a decent plan."

"You'll be careful?"

He eyed her more closely then. "Are you worried?"

"It occurred to me that if your neighbor is smuggling birds and probably eggs out of the country, he'll be asking top dollar. He won't want to lose his lucrative income. Are you sure the men weren't carrying weapons?"

"None I saw, but I take your point. Don't worry. Nikolai and I are professionals. We won't take stupid risks. We'll nose around and if we find anything incriminating, we'll call in the authorities."

Ella yawned before she could cover her mouth.

"You're tired. Let's go to bed."

"Okay, but try not to hit me this time. My jaw is still sore."

Dillon stilled, the color fading from his cheeks. He jerked away from her. "I should head home."

"No." Aw, crap. Her and her big mouth. "Dillon, look at me." She encouraged him to face her by cupping his jaw. "You didn't mean to do it. *I. Know. This.* You had a bad dream and struck out. Please, come to bed."

He hesitated then gave a brief nod.

"I'd like to get the alpaca fleece you promised me because a local lady is giving lessons. I noticed the flyer at a local cafe. Although I don't know how easy it will be carting it around the landslide. Can I go back with you for a day or two?"

A frown marched across Dillon's face.

"What if I promise to stay around the house? You'll be there and your brother-in-law."

"I'll consider it."

"Okay," Ella said and stood. "If you want a shower, the towels are in the hall cupboard just opposite. Help yourself. I bought a new toothbrush last week. It's in the bathroom cabinet still in its packet. Your beard looks distinguished now. It suits you."

"Does it make me sexy enough to warrant a goodnight kiss?"

"As long as you clean your teeth. We both ate garlic tonight."

Dillon chuckled. "You go first. I want a glass of water."

She nodded and hurried off to get ready for bed. Normally, she wore a long T-shirt but tonight she decided on nothing except a dab of her favorite perfume. Yes, she was tired. Yes, every muscle in her body warbled a song of misery, but she'd need to be a saint to resist this gruff and sometimes bad-tempered military man.

Besides, didn't sex—the excellent kind—flood the body with endorphins and aid sleep?

That was a cure she craved this night.

9

THINGS START TO MAKE SENSE

DILLON SLIPPED INTO THE bed cautiously, thankful that Ella had a large version rather than a single. He could've slept on the couch or in her spare room, but something drove him to seek her comfort. Normally, sharing a bed with a woman meant sex, but with Ella, the need for closeness drove him. Which made no sense, but he was a man who listened to his gut instincts. They'd saved him more than once.

"Dillon?"

"If it's someone else, we're in trouble."

"Cold."

She scooched nearer and wound around him like a clinging vine. Her bare breasts pressed against his chest while her limbs entwined with his.

She yawned. "Thought I could do sex. Later. So tired."

The coolness of her flesh did little to calm the burst of

desire that grabbed him by the balls when she crooned the word *sex*. Tension slid through his arms, and in self-defense, he ran through the steps of his upcoming mission. *Huh!* His mind automatically turned soldier on him. Even though he'd tossed a few ideas around his mind, he still hadn't decided on the best course of action. He'd discuss it with Nikolai. If his brother-in-law suggested he report this to the police and step away, he'd follow the advice.

His mother's adage about borrowing trouble held wisdom.

With that decision made, he could no longer distract himself from the woman in his arms. She'd fallen asleep and her small, puffing breaths tickled his chest. A smile curved his lips as satisfaction settled over him. He closed his own eyes and relaxed.

On the edge of dropping into slumber, the whisper of his name dragged him back to wakefulness.

"Dillon."

The hairs on his arms stood to attention.

"Dillon."

Crap. He slipped from the bed and tiptoed to the kitchen. While he waited for something to happen, he poured himself a glass of water. He sipped, his gaze prowling the darkness. Impatience stalked him. He was a practical man who preferred control. He understood the things in front of his face.

This was beyond his pay grade.

"I can't believe this. If that is you, Hana, you need to stop harassing Ella. Why are you hanging around here?

Dammit, you're one of the good ones. A saint, and you sure as hell didn't deserve to die alone in the house. I'm so sorry. I assumed you'd be safe." Dillon paused his throat tight. He moistened his mouth with the water. It didn't help.

He lost track of how long he stood in the dark kitchen, waiting for something, anything to happen.

Hana's excitement and enthusiasm had made him laugh. A fresh start in a place that didn't have war and people didn't go around brandishing guns. A safe home. It was all Hana had wanted.

Epic fuckin' fail.

Seven months after her arrival, she'd been dead.

Despite modern communication, he hadn't received the news for almost three weeks. Too late to attend her funeral. And worse, she'd died alone. The reports he'd read and a chat to the local cops told him she hadn't gone easy. She'd given whoever attacked her hell. Unfortunately, the DNA hadn't helped the investigation.

"If you're intending to haunt me the least you could do is tell me what happened. Give me something so I can catch these bastards."

"Who are you talking to?"

The light flicked on, and he blinked to acclimatize. Ella tightened the belt of her dressing gown, but not before she flashed her breasts.

"Nice." He winked at her, his gaze pointed.

"Don't change the subject. Who were you talking to?"

"Your friendly ghost. I don't get it. If she wants something, why the hell doesn't she ask and be done with it? Hints are for the birds."

Ella yawned wide. "You're a fine one to talk. Soldier men, according to your mother, are terrible at conversations. When the discussion becomes uncomfortable, you grunt or say you don't want to deliberate on the topic."

Dillon snorted. Sounded like something his mother would say.

"Or snort," Ella added. "Now that I know you're breaking the soldier rules and having a conversation." She did quote marks in the air. "I'm going back to bed. Keep the friendly ghost busy and I might get a few hours of solid sleep."

Dillon watched Ella as she shuffled from sight. Or more accurately, his gaze hooked onto her curvy arse. A sigh escaped once she'd disappeared from view because his mind had jumped straight to sex. That was plain wrong when she was in pain from her injuries and sported a bruise on her face because of him.

Soon, he'd head back to his team. Ella was a complication he didn't need.

Best to concentrate on the bird thing, get it sorted and leave as he'd originally intended.

Safer for everyone.

· ♥ · ♥ · ♥ · ♥ · ♥ ·

DILLON HAD LEFT BY the time she woke the next morning. He'd left a note.

Thanks for dinner. Take care. Dillon.

132

Ella scowled. Honestly. Was it too much to ask for more details? Like was he going to visit again, for instance? She slammed the coffee cannister on the countertop. She was all for brevity but there was a time and a place. Dillon Williams... *Grrr!* He made her crazy.

She stomped over to her electric kettle, her aches and pains taking time to make themselves felt through her temper. *Ow. Ow. Ow.*

"Dillon Williams, this friends with benefits is not working for me. You can take your benefits and stuff them somewhere else."

·❤·❤·❤·❤·❤·

DILLON STILLED AT THE sound of an approaching motor vehicle. All the locals were aware of the landslide blocking the road, so why was someone driving up here?

He turned, and his sister leaned out of the passenger window and wolf-whistled. Dillon shook his head and waved. His younger sister was just as crazy as ever. Although his mother would deny this and blame her husband, Dillon suspected Summer took after their mother. Local rumor said his mother had been wild in her younger days.

Nikolai pulled alongside. "You didn't have to come to meet us."

Dillon gave his brother-in-law a one-fingered salute, and Nikolai grinned, his brown eyes sparkling in his tan face, indicative of his Māori heritage. His brother-in-law irritated him too. In fact, Nikolai needled him on purpose to get a response. A wry smile etched into his face, digging deep enough for him to feel the stretch. The ribbing usually worked, too.

There was a time when he would've punched Nikolai's nose rather than restraining the impulse.

Dillon approached the vehicle—a rental they'd collected in Palmerston North. "Mum is excited. She didn't expect you this early though."

"Tell me about it," Summer said through the open window. "She rang me three times yesterday and texted me this morning about what to buy at the supermarket and what did the baby need. You owe me, Dillon. Not only am I bringing manpower, but I'm also distracting our mother and putting myself in the way of umpteen lectures."

His sister had always been pretty, but marriage and motherhood agreed with her. Her chubbiness had reduced into sexy curves while her eyes glowed with happiness.

Nikolai climbed out and strode around the front of the vehicle. A big, strong man, he stretched out his hand. "Good to see you, bro."

He shook Nikolai's hand then drew him in for a man hug. "Noted," Dillon said once he pulled back. "What are you going to tell Mum when she asks about Nikolai?"

"That Nikolai wanted to check out the landslide and your place. I'll tell him you need help with...with... I'll tell her it's secret SAS stuff. She'll be nosy but I'll plead ignorance and divert her with Sam. Anything else, I'll wing it." Summer winked at Nikolai. "I'm excellent at using initiative."

"You are, sweetheart." Nikolai opened the vehicle for

his wife and closed the door once she'd climbed out. He opened the rear door and bent over to kiss his son. "Behave." He kissed his son's black curls again before dragging out a daypack and shrugging it onto his shoulders. "I'm leaving my sat-phone with Summer."

"I have mine. Summer, did you learn anything else on the black web?"

"I'm still researching. Hopefully, I can leave Sam to Mum and pretend I'm napping. She'll accept that excuse."

Dillon grimaced. "Mum is usually a step ahead of us."

"Grandsons are excellent distractions." Summer wrapped her arms around Nikolai's neck and kissed him.

Their closeness and strong love made Dillon uncomfortable, and he turned away. His mind jogged to Ella. Sassy and forthright. Sexy and fun. He clenched his hands and attempted to shake her free. Like a tick—an unwelcome parasite—thoughts of her clung with determination.

"Do you have a plan?" Nikolai asked once Summer drove away.

"I figured we'd do a recon tonight. This afternoon, I can show you the traps I've sighted. I want to repair my boundary anyway, so we'll go armed with fencing gear."

"Did they have guards posted?"

"Nah, not that I noticed. I figure they won't worry much with the road blocked. No one with any sense will visit their place."

Nikolai slanted him a look, his dark brows cocked. "You saying I have no sense?"

"If the hat fits." Dillon maintained a straight face with

effort.

"You're trying to wind me up. I can feel the key in my back."

Dillon chuckled.

"You okay? Your head in the right place?"

Dillon's amusement died. His shoulders stiffened. "I'm fine."

"Yeah, that's what you told Summer. Tell me." Nikolai's voice held a challenge. "Josh thinks it's something else. He said your head wasn't in the game."

A harsh sigh worked up his throat. He'd promised himself he'd seek help once he arrived home. He hadn't. Instead, he'd wallowed until Ella burst into his life. He trained his gaze on the ground. He told himself it was to watch his footing. *Big, fat liar.* It was so he'd miss Nikolai's reaction, although his brother-in-law wasn't stupid.

"Hana," he said in a heavy voice. "I failed her. She died."

Nikolai squeezed his shoulder and kept walking. "Hana wouldn't want you to knock yourself out like this. She loved you."

"Yeah," Dillon said hoarsely. That was part of the problem. "I didn't love her."

"Were you screwing around on her?"

"What? No, I told you all this during our phone call. Besides, when did I have time?"

"It bears repeating, because you're wallowing in the past. Did Hana realize you didn't feel the same way?"

Dillon sighed. "Yeah, she knew. She hoped I'd change my mind."

"And in another recap, why did you get married if you

didn't feel the same way?"

"It was the only way she could come to New Zealand. She was in danger in Afghanistan. The New Zealand government was being an arsehole about letting her into the country. But worse, she fuckin' died in New Zealand in a senseless bloody home invasion."

"I'm sorry, man. It sucks."

"That's why I need to understand what's going on here. For Hana. If these guys are stealing birds and selling them to collectors, they need to be stopped. She'd be appalled if she knew." He hesitated to tell Nikolai about the ghost. His brother-in-law would call in the medical folk if he learned of Dillon's ghost. Hell, he'd do the same if Ella wasn't suffering the same delusions.

"I take it you have a plan?"

"They have cameras. I've found a couple but I might have missed some when I was blundering around clueless."

"We won't have the element of surprise." Nikolai frowned. "Summer will be upset if I get hurt."

"The knee better? You're not limping."

"Physio signed off ages ago. It's almost one hundred percent, but my life is easier now that I'm training men rather than on active duty. Summer likes having me home more often. Did you know she's writing a book? A romance."

"Summer has always had her nose in a book."

"Not always," Nikolai said with a grin.

"Don't!" Dillon barked. "No more about my sister's sex life."

"We can talk about yours. Your mother mentioned Ella

several times."

"Ella?"

"Marlene is matchmaking."

"Ella is a friend. That's all."

Nikolai shot him a look as they reached the blocked road.

"A friend," Dillon repeated.

"Whatever you say. Hell, it will take a while for them to clear this. It looks as if more of the hill could go."

"Ella's car is under there."

Nikolai stared at the scar on the hillside and the mountainous pile of earth blocking the road. "She's lucky she's alive."

"Yeah."

After a brisk walk, they arrived at his house.

"I wasn't sure what to expect after your mother's complaints you live miles from her," Nikolai said.

"The only reason I chose Eketahuna was for Hana to have family close. We both loved this place when we first saw it. Dad likes getting out here too. He looks after the alpacas and the dog for me when I'm not at home. Says it gives him an interest. You hungry?"

"I am, but first show me these alpacas of yours."

Dillon greeted Rufus with a rigorous head scratch and dinner while Nikolai released the alpacas from their night shelter.

"Are you keeping them indoors every night?" Nikolai asked, a faint smile on his face as he watched the animals trot outside to their paddock. Rufus scampered after a rabbit.

"Only while the weather is wet. They're capable of living outdoors, but Hana and I decided if we handled them often they'd be easier to deal with for shearing, drenching, and vet visits."

"They're cute." Nikolai fished out a cell phone and snapped photos. "I'll send them to Jake and Louie." His dark brows lifted. "Want to pose with one?"

"No," Dillon snapped.

Chores completed, Dillon led Nikolai inside to the kitchen.

"Bacon and eggs do?"

"Yep. I'll make the coffee."

One thing he liked about Nikolai. He pulled his weight and helped Summer around the house. Despite his initial fears, this man was perfect for his adventurous sister. And just like that, his thoughts slid to another woman with attitude.

The distant *whop-whop* of a helicopter saved him this time.

"Crap." Dillon strode outside with Nikolai behind him.

"Is that landing at the neighbor's place?"

"Yeah. It arrives around once a week, sometimes more often, but the time varies."

"Have we missed our window of opportunity?" Nikolai asked.

"We'll check out the place tonight, anyway."

They chatted while they ate breakfast.

"Jake hooked up with that hippie chick," Dillon said.

"She doesn't resemble any hippie I've met," Nikolai said. "She's also crazy wealthy now. Jake grumbles about being a kept man."

"He's retired though. I'm sure Josh told me that."

"Yeah, he trained as a cop and is working for the Sloan Police force. Says there is all sorts of crazy happening in the town. He swears he saw a UFO last week."

Dillon barked out a laugh. "What was he drinking?"

"He swears he'd been on duty all afternoon and had drunk nothing stronger than coffee. I asked for photos but he said shock struck, he dropped his phone and the UFO disappeared before he recovered it."

After Dillon stacked the dishes in the sink to do later, he grabbed the camera and tucked a gun in the small of his back.

"Do we need weapons? I didn't bring mine because we flew."

"A precaution."

He led Nikolai out to his shed where he collected a hammer and staples and shoved them in a day pack before grabbing three posts.

"You want me to carry something?"

"Another three or four posts."

Dillon strode the slight incline and led Nikolai into the cool of the bush. Fine weather for a change. Lately, rain dominated the weather forecast. Water saturated the ground and mud splattered Nikolai's pristine boots. That amused Dillon.

They took half an hour to reach the boundary fence.

"The first of the cameras is here on the right. It's high in the tree and blends." Dillon lowered his voice because he wasn't sure who was around.

"Bit of a cheek trapping on your land," Nikolai murmured, jerking his head in a silent indication he'd spotted the camera.

"I guess they decided I was gone for most of the time and it wouldn't be an issue. My presence will create problems, especially since I've started birdwatching."

Nikolai snorted. "Have you spotted a kiwi in the wild?"

"When I was a kid." Dillon yawned. "Josh and I went camping with the scouts. If we're lucky, we might hear one call tonight. They're hard to spot because their color blends."

"Not sleeping?"

"Have been lately." The truth. Ella had helped in with this apart from the night he'd punched her. "You have nightmares?"

"Used to. Not so much now. You?"

Dillon grunted, the sound enough of an answer.

Nikolai froze. "What's that bird?"

Dillon followed his gaze. "A kokako. They're rare, but the population is growing in this area because of the sanctuary at Mt. Bruce. You should get Summer to take you to visit. Mum will babysit Sam. She is friends with the workers and you might wrangle a private tour. Ella works there, but she's off until Monday."

"You're not one to mention a woman so often," Nikolai said, his tone innocent.

"She reminds me of Summer."

"Interesting." Nikolai's lips twitched.

Dillon's first instinct was to lash out. He resisted. Barely. Instead, he dumped his posts. "This is the boundary fence with Pukaha Mt. Bruce."

"You checked over there?" Nikolai dropped his posts too.

"Found a few traps. We'll check on them now."

"No cameras here?"

"Haven't noticed any."

Nikolai nodded. Dillon vaulted the fence, and Nikolai followed suit. Both scanned their surroundings—thick trees with a vast array of ferns and saplings beneath. Not much sunlight reached the ground below the canopy. Thick leaf litter cushioned their footsteps, not that they bumbled around. Instinctively, they slipped into soldier-mode and stepped noiselessly through the trees. They paused frequently, listening for other trespassers or voices and scanning for cameras and bird traps. Communication was hand signals, and Dillon was pleased to have Nikolai along. Someone to watch his back, and he'd guard Nikolai in return. Summer would gut him if anything happened to her husband.

Dillon spotted the trap he'd noticed previously and halted. He pointed it out to Nikolai. They discovered six more although none of them contained birds. Nikolai snapped several photos.

By common consent, they retreated to the spot where they'd left the fencing gear.

"The photos should be enough to get action from the sanctuary and the cops," Nikolai murmured. "My gut tells me your instincts are right. There is something shady going on here."

"It burns me they're getting away with poaching birds."

"We'll stop them. Let's get this fence of yours mended. You going to run stock here?"

"I'll need to once I expand. I have one hundred hectares in total."

"Are you retiring soon?"

Dillon's thoughts slipped to Ella. "No."

"Just asking," Nikolai said in a mild voice. "You'll know when you're ready."

If he didn't get killed first. Neither of them voiced this, but Dillon was certain they both thought it. Soldiering in Afghanistan held risk.

With Nikolai's help, he removed the rotten posts and dug in new ones. Not perfect since he didn't own strainers to tighten the wire but alpaca proof.

"I'll play birdwatcher during our return," Dillon said.

Nikolai stared at Dillon then nodded. "I could take photos to show Summer. She hasn't visited your place. Find me birds, bro."

They ambled back to the farmhouse, stopping often and coincidentally near cameras to photograph birds and the scenery.

"Toasted sandwich okay for lunch?" Dillon asked.

"Yeah. Do you have a laptop? I'll download the photos from your camera while you make me lunch."

Dillon jerked his head toward the passage. "Hana's laptop is in the wardrobe."

"Summer told me the place was trashed."

Dillon opened the fridge and pulled out a loaf of bread. "I found it in the shed where the alpacas sleep."

"Why did Hana leave the laptop there?"

"She wanted to document everything about the alpacas. She took photos and used the computer to keep records."

"Have you turned it on?"

"No, I don't bother going online unless I'm in town or at the family home. I use my phone."

Nikolai disappeared and reappeared with a laptop case. While Dillon grated cheese, chopped tomatoes and arranged ham on slices of bread, Nikolai plugged in the laptop and turned it on.

"Password?"

"It was Hana's laptop. I've no idea."

Nikolai tried several words then grinned. "Hana had a sense of humor and determination."

"What's her password?"

"I Love Dillon Williams."

"How the hell did you pick that?"

"Lucky guess."

"Crap," Dillon said, guilt swamping him. "Am I a bad person for not loving her? I liked her, enjoyed spending time with her."

"You gave Hana a chance of a better life," Nikolai said. "Stop beating yourself up. You weren't here and Hana's death was because of the arseholes who invaded your home. It's not your fault. Logically, you understand that, but you're twisted with guilt because Hana loved you and you didn't return the sentiment."

Nikolai tapped several keys and made a humming sound.

Dillon checked the sandwiches before opening the camera and handing Nikolai the card.

"There's already a card in the laptop." Nikolai clicked several keys and photos of birds popped on the screen.

Dillon peered over Nikolai's shoulder. "Hana took photos of the traps. She knew about the birds." There were several shots of men, but he recognized none of them. "Has she saved any photos to the laptop already?"

Nikolai clicked through the various files and picked one to open. "She's written notes of what she saw. Days. Dates. She mentions a helicopter."

"We need to look in that shed."

Nikolai glanced at him, his impassive soldier visage—the one he saw on his own face when he was about to go on a mission. "Here's an idea. What if Hana's death wasn't a simple home invasion? What if she stuck her nose into this, and they took action?"

Dillon grunted, yet that was where his mind had trekked. Now that they'd found Hana's notes, the situation made more sense.

"What do you want to do?"

"I intend to check the shed before we go to the cops. I'd hate to let these bastards get away with Hana's murder."

"Do you have any cop friends? We can't go in guns blazing without causing ourselves trouble and a lot of paperwork."

A sigh escaped him because Nikolai was right. "I'll talk to Ella. She'll know the local cops."

"Or you could ring the cops yourself."

Another excellent point. If Hana's death had occurred because of the poaching of native birds, the last thing he wanted was to get Ella involved.

At eleven that night, he and Nikolai drifted through the bush, the night vision goggles that Nikolai had packed made the journey easier. A gun snugged into the base of his spine, and he'd shoved his favorite folding knife in his pocket. Not that he intended to use either weapon. This was an in and out situation. A recon to gather information. He'd also packed a selection of tools and items he might require to break into a locked building, and he carried these in a daypack.

His neighbor's farm lay in darkness as they skulked toward it. Dillon led Nikolai straight to the shed where he suspected they kept the birds contained. To his surprise, the door wasn't locked this time. He applied CRC to the door hinges and cautiously opened it. Cages of different sizes filled one wall, but each was empty. Dillon glanced at Nikolai who snapped photos. Dillon spotted a feather on the ground and scooped it up for closer observation.

After an exchange of hand signals, they slipped out of the shed and closed the door again. They glided from one shadow to the next, checking for cameras before they moved. Most of the cameras protected the shed from intruders.

Three vehicles. Engines all cold. Dillon hadn't met his neighbor recently. On his arrival home, the idea of doing the polite social thing had turned him nauseous. Now, a visit might appear suspicious, especially if they'd caught him on one of their cameras.

He signaled a retreat, and they slinked through the shadows, moving with purpose until they reached the tree line.

"Opinion?" Dillon asked.

"With the things Hana has documented, you have enough to go to the cops. More than a suspicion. The only thing I don't like is their empty shed. Will the charges stick if they have no birds in their possession?"

Nikolai was right. It was time to bring in the cops.

10

THE GHOST SINGS A WARNING

"Ella. Ella. Ella."

Ella pulled her pillow over her head and tried to block the persistent sound. She'd spent an enjoyable evening with Summer, Dillon's sister, who had invited her to go to the local pub for drinks. Although her aches and pains were retreating, she still felt physically drained and had hoped she'd sleep well. Not happening.

"Ella. Ella. Ella."

A cold wash of air on her forearms—the ones holding the pillow in place—pebbled chill bumps over her flesh.

"Leave me alone. I've done everything you wanted. I visited Dillon and can't do anything more."

Ella gave up trying to sleep and read a book about spinning alpaca fleece before switching to the latest Ilona Andrews urban fantasy. When the ghostly whispers and the wafts of icy air kept blasting her, she dressed rapidly in leggings and a sweater.

She wandered to the kitchen without bothering to switch on a light. A glance at the microwave clock had her scowling. 5:45.

A creak and the breaking of glass had her freezing in the midst of reaching for the kettle.

"Ella, hide!"

Ella's pulse leaped like a startled rabbit. Fear left her mouth dry, her throat tight. *Hide.* She scuttled into her bedroom, saw the unmade bed and almost panicked. If she arranged the covers and made it look as if she hadn't been here overnight. Yes, that might work. And if she breathed in, she might manage to slide underneath. The covers were long and would hide the gap. They might not think to look under the bed.

Low voices toward the front of the house had her moving at double-quick time. She yanked the quilt cover into place and smoothed out the impression of her head. At the last second, she turned over the pillow so it was flat before she dropped to the floor and forced her body into the gap.

Not a second too soon.

Footsteps in the passage indicated someone was walking toward her bedroom. The footsteps sounded masculine to her, the strides long and purposeful. She caught a flicker of light from the corner of her eye and wished she'd grabbed her phone. It was charging right now. Hopefully, they didn't spot it and think she was at home.

"No one here."

The second set of footsteps approached and stopped by

her bed. "Where is she?"

"How the hell do I know? I saw her in the pub tonight with another woman. The barman told me it was Williams's sister."

"What's she doing here?"

"A visit home."

The man supplying the answers sounded pissed, but Ella wasn't sure if it was because of his friend's nosy questions or the fact she wasn't there.

"What are we going to do now?"

"Wreck the place and hope we distract Williams because his girlfriend's house got burgled. That's what the boss wanted. Grab a few valuables. We need to make this look like a robbery."

Ella pressed her hand against her mouth to muffle her cry of protest.

"It's like an icebox in here. Let's get this finished, then we can go home."

Something crashed against her bedroom wall. Ella flinched at the harsh noise.

"Whoa!" one man said. "Did you see that?"

"What?"

"You didn't notice that book sail across the room and hit the wall?"

"Stop mucking around. We don't wanna get caught."

"I'll do the lounge and kitchen. I wonder if she has food. I'm starving." Judging by his footsteps, he sprinted from her bedroom.

Drawers opened and closed. Ella winced at the harsh rip of fabric and listened for her wardrobe door, her terror giving way to anger. If this idiot started destroying her vintage dresses—the ones she'd collected for years—she'd commit murder herself.

The door of her wardrobe opened with a strident creak.

Ella was ready to cast aside caution and let rip with whatever weapon came to hand when the man cried out. "What the fuck?"

An object thudded against the wall. Another crashed on the floor.

Rapid footsteps thumped from her room and retreated.

"This place is freaky," a male voice said, his register higher than it had been earlier.

"Told you."

"I'm outta here."

"I'm not staying here alone."

The temperature in her bedroom rose rapidly, and Ella slid out of hiding. She cautiously stood and cocked her head. Screams came from near her front door. This was one time when close neighbors might have proved helpful. The screams grew in pitch and plates smashed against something hard.

Then silence fell.

A vehicle accelerated, the gears grinding as the driver attempted to haul arse. More silence when the only sound was her own breathing.

Ella worried her bottom lip. Was it safe? She needed to grab her phone and ring the cops.

"Ella. Ella. Ella."

Her ghost whispered, the sound of her name strangely soothing.

SHELLEY MUNRO

Ella crept through her house, her ears peeled for any sound out of order. Once she reached the kitchen, she checked the clock on the microwave. The appliance wasn't telling the time any longer since it lay upside down near the counter. She risked turning on a light. Shards of pottery, tea bags, and her potted herbs littered the floor.

Nearer the fridge, eggs decorated the tiles, several with yolks still intact. The home invaders had upended her cutlery drawer and dumped the contents of her cannisters of flour and sugar near the pantry.

With a held breath, Ella checked her phone. They had seen it but hadn't clicked she might be at home. Luckily for her. One of the men had ripped it from the charger, and it had landed on the floor. The screen had a crack diagonally across the middle.

"Please work. Please work." Ella powered up her cell phone, a harsh exhalation of relief exiting with a whoosh. She dialed 111 and told the operator she wanted the police.

"Are you in danger?" the operator asked.

"I don't think so."

"Stay on the line. The police are on their way."

Five minutes later, a car entered her driveway. The red-and-blue flashing lights boosted her courage.

"They're here. Thank you." Ella ended the call.

She hurried to meet the two constables, both of whom she knew since they were around her age. Connor was a tall blond with serious muscles the uniform didn't hide. The local women called him Viking while his partner was a diminutive Asian girl by the name of Molly. She'd transferred from Wellington two years ago.

"Ella, I near had a heart attack when we were called here." Molly gave her a quick hug. "Are you okay?"

"I'm fine. I hid under the bed and they didn't realize I was there."

"Did you recognize them?" Connor asked.

"No, but I'd distinguish their voices if I heard them again."

"Did they take anything?" Molly asked.

"I haven't noticed anything missing. My kitchen is a mess. My bedroom too. They enjoyed chucking things around to cause maximum damage."

Ella showed the two cops through her house. The lounge had cushions tossed and a chair lay on its side. Her collection of DVDs fanned across the floor, but the damage was superficial.

"They ripped some of my clothes. I was set to show myself and do bodily harm if they'd started on the dresses in my wardrobe."

"I don't blame you," Molly said. "Your vintage clothes are gorgeous."

Connor took photos of the damage. "Are you sure there is nothing missing?"

"Everything seems to be here."

"They did a number on your underwear." Connor lifted a brow. "A suitor scorned?"

"*Pffft!* Oh!" Ella said as she stared at the remnants of a black cardigan with embroidered red flowers decorating the sleeves. It was one of her favorites and they'd ruined the garment.

Car lights illuminated the exterior and both cops tensed.

"Wait here," Connor said.

He reappeared a few minutes later with Summer in tow.

"Ella!" Summer said. "Connor said someone broke into your house. Are you all right?"

"I'm still jumpy and I'm pissed they've destroyed my favorite cardigan. It was a one of a kind. What are you doing up this early?"

"I volunteered to do a bakery run. Sam is teething and kept everyone awake last night," Summer said. "Once you're done here, pack a bag. You can stay with Dillon. I'm driving to meet him and Nikolai before I head back to Mum's and Dad's place."

"Stay elsewhere for a couple of days," Molly said. "We'll drive past at random times and keep an eye out for any activity."

Connor filled out a form and handed it to her. "An incident report for your insurance company."

Ella grimaced. "They will love me. First, my car and now my house is broken into and my possessions trashed."

"Could've been worse," Connor said, his expression hard. "They might have discovered you hiding under the bed. It was smart making your bed look as if you hadn't slept in it."

The police left and Summer turned to her, brisk and as managing as her mother. "Pack a bag and we'll get moving. I'm already late, and Nikolai will be worried. These military men work on precise time." She winked at Ella. "Something for you to remember."

"Dillon and I are friends. We're in the move right along, nothing to see here category."

154

Summer laughed. "Really? And I thought you were both in the doth protest too much slot. Ha! Your cheeks are turning red. I knew it."

It was a short drive to the spot where the landslide blocked the road. Summer had a lead foot, but Ella had to admit the woman possessed driving skills.

When they arrived Dillon and Nikolai were waiting for them, both big men pacing.

"Ha! I told you they'd be stressed."

But Ella wasn't listening to Summer. Instead, she stared at Dillon whose expression had blanked when he spied her. His dark brows pulled together and she'd bet if she stood closer, she'd spot the giveaway tic in his jaw. This man was *not* pleased with her presence.

Summer climbed out of the car, and Ella followed suit, albeit at a much slower pace.

"What is she doing here?" Dillon demanded.

Nikolai and Summer exchanged a glance before turning their attention on Dillon. Ella swallowed and had to stop herself from retreating a step.

"I told her to come," Summer said, her tone way too innocent. Anyone with half a brain would suspect her of messing with her brother.

Ella opened her mouth to protest, but an ugly croak escaped instead of explanations.

Dillon scowled. "Well, you can take her home again. I don't want her here."

"Now that was plain rude," Summer said. "And I brought you food too, you ungrateful lout. You wait until I tell Mum."

SHELLEY MUNRO

A muffled snort came from Nikolai. Dillon's scowl grew blacker while Summer winked at her husband. Ella was certain the word she mouthed was *payback*.

"I'll go," Ella said, her gut churning with disappointment. "I can stay with one of my other friends."

Dillon's gaze shifted from Ella to Summer and back. It drilled through her, and absurdly, the first stages of arousal frisked her body. "Why can't you stay in your house?"

"Someone broke in this morning," Summer said.

Dillon closed the distance between them and placed his hands on Ella's shoulders. "Are you all right? Did they hurt you?"

"She hid under the bed," Summer said with approval.

"Will you let Ella talk?" Dillon snapped.

"Sorry. Shutting up now." Summer made a zipping motion across her mouth.

Dillon scowled at his sister before turning to Nikolai. "You don't spank her enough."

"He doesn't spank me at all," Summer said in a sweet voice.

Dillon grunted. "His mistake."

"I behave for Nikolai as a perfect wife should."

This time Nikolai snorted, and Summer's sassy wink zapped to Ella.

"Tell us about the people who broke into your place," Dillon said.

"I'd better go," Summer said. "Before Mum packs us off home. Sam howled for most of the night. Another tooth," she said to Nikolai.

Nikolai kissed Summer, and they spoke in undertones

with Summer asking the odd question before nodding.

Dillon distracted her. "Are you okay?" he asked in a gruff voice. "Did they hurt you?"

"They had no idea I was at home. Summer and I went to the pub for drinks. One of them mentioned seeing me there, and they assumed I'd stayed overnight with her. My car was in the driveway. Um..." She glanced at Nikolai and Summer. When it was clear they were focused on each other, Ella turned back to Dillon. "The ghost warned me. I was awake already because she kept yammering and blowing cold air over me. I'd dressed and when I heard glass breaking, I yanked up my bedcovers to make the bed appear unused and crawled underneath. From what I can gather, the ghost scared them off, but not before they did more damage. Once I was certain they'd gone, I called the cops and they arrived within five minutes."

"Did you mention the ghost to the cops?"

"Do I look crazy?"

A slow smile curled across his face, making him appear more approachable. "No, you look gorgeous." He tugged a lock of pink hair.

"Can I stay with you?"

"Yeah, but you need to stay close to the house."

"Have you found something?"

"Yes and no. Nikolai is giving the information to Summer. It's time to take what we have to the cops."

"Dillon, there is something else. It sounded as if they wanted to grab me specifically because they *were* pissed when they didn't find me. They mentioned you."

"Crap. That changes things. Tell me exactly what they

said. Did you tell the cops this?"

"No. I just reported the break-in."

"Better tell Summer, and she can tell the cops."

Ella wrinkled her nose. "Molly and Connor won't be happy with me for withholding information."

"They'll get over it." Dillon took her hand and hauled her toward Nikolai and Summer. He maintained his grip and heat roared along her arm.

Ella risked a glance at Summer and got hit with a teasing smile. Still, Dillon didn't release her hand.

"The break-in at Ella's place has something to do with the birds and Hana's murder," Dillon said. "Summer, you need to tell the cops that. It's connected, but make sure they wait two days before they do anything. It looks as if they've shipped out the birds they had on hand. If they go in today, there won't be any evidence."

"What will you do now?" Summer asked.

"We'll stake out a trap and photograph them removing the birds," Dillon said.

"I'm helping." Ella lifted her chin. "I refuse to stay in the house."

"You're right," Dillon said unexpectedly. "You'll be with me like a tick on a dog. Close."

Summer sniffed. "Dillon, if that's all the sweet-talk you have it's no wonder you're alone."

"I'm alone because these bastards murdered my wife when she got too close to their lucrative operation," Dillon snapped.

Ella flinched his words like a slap. That sure put her in her place and halted any ideas of happy ever after.

11

THE STING

ELLA SITUATED ONE OF the daypacks full of food on her shoulders, grabbed her overnight bag and waited while the two men took possession of the larger packs.

"I'll take that for you," Dillon said, snatching her overnight bag from her before she could protest. He stormed off, leaving Nikolai and Ella alone.

"Don't mind Grumpy," Nikolai said with a lazy grin. "I ignore him. It's best if you do too."

Ella gave an imperceptible nod of understanding and set off after Dillon. He powered away with his long legs, but she didn't try to maintain his speed. The man drove her crazy with his snapping and snarling. He had a softer side. She'd witnessed it, savored it during their lovemaking. Right now, however, a sane woman would take one peek and flee. She wished she could walk away, but thoughts of him had filled her mind since their last meeting.

Each time she tried to shove him out, he returned, helped in part by the friendly ghost since the pair had become entwined in her mind.

A dose of his bad temper might cure her once and for all.

Dillon pushed his legs faster, eager for the pulse of muscles and the rapid pump of his heart that told him he was alive. It was his fault those men had invaded Ella's home. He'd placed her in danger.

He paused, his mind busy with the angles. How the devil had they learned he and Ella were friends? Two possibilities. One—someone had watched him either arrive or leave Ella's place. Two—Ella had told someone and word had spread around the district of Eketahuna.

No, a third option. The neighbor had placed a camera on his property to record his comings and goings. He cursed under his breath, wishing he'd thought of this before, because if this proved correct, Ella was in danger again.

When he arrived back at his vehicle, he dumped his pack and Ella's overnight bag in the back. By this time, Nikolai and Ella approached the vehicle.

"Ella, did you tell anyone you were with me?" he asked.

"Only that I stayed during the storm until I could get out safely. Are you accusing me of gossip? What was I meant to tell people?"

"I'm worried about why these guys hassled you to get at me."

"I don't gossip." Her voice emerged as crisp as a drill sergeant's dress uniform. The slight tilt of her nose as it lifted higher in the air made his lips twitch. He resisted the humor with difficulty.

"I wondered if the neighbor is spying on me," Dillon said. "Not at the house but near the driveway where I mightn't notice a camera."

Nikolai frowned. "Hana caused them problems. It would make sense for them to keep an eye on her."

"They murdered her, didn't they?" Ella asked.

"That's our suspicion," Nikolai said.

"Maybe that's why she's hanging around," Dillon murmured.

He caught Nikolai's incredulous expression.

"Ask Ella why she drove out to visit me the first time. The day the landslide came down," Dillon said.

Nikolai stored the rest of the bags in the back, and Ella stuffed herself in the remaining gap. Nikolai climbed in the front.

"Hana has been haunting me. She spends her time between my cottage and here, and she has been driving me batty. I'm not getting much sleep."

"Unless you're with me," Dillon said.

"One plus for you," Ella quipped.

Nikolai chuckled. "You're pulling my leg."

"Does his face look as if he's telling lies?" Ella asked, indicating the somber Dillon. "And you can ask the two guys who broke into my house last night. She scared the crap out of them with her wailing and tossing things across the room. If it wasn't for Hana, the pair would've stayed a lot longer."

Dillon drove to his property, and once the house came

161

into sight, he scanned for cameras.

"Hell," Nikolai said. "You're right. There is a camera in that tree. It's pointing toward your house."

"How would that work? Is it battery operated?" Ella asked.

"My guess is it's on a motion sensor," Nikolai said.

"I don't see any others." Dillon coasted to a stop outside his house. "One is probably enough to make certain I'm away from the house."

"No, there'll be another one somewhere," Nikolai said. "Around the back, because they'd want notice of when you're near the boundary fence. A second camera would lessen the chances of discovery."

"We should inform the cops." Dillon tapped his fingers on the steering wheel.

"These people are well-organized," Nikolai said. They have to be with the big money involved. How are we going to catch them?"

"Somehow, we need to locate any cameras spying on us and stop them recording. They probably have them set up to send a notification to their cell phones."

"That's plain creepy." Ella stiffened, her voice rising in pitch.

Once they searched for cameras, they were easier to spot. They found three around his house plus the initial one Nikolai had spotted.

"And that answers your question about how they knew to hit Ella's place," Nikolai said. "You two groped each other outdoors."

Hell. He had. She had. A scowl attached to his mouth

and dug deep. His hands fisted. The way they'd taken something private between him and Ella and recorded it brought a sense of violation.

"Suggestions?" he asked Nikolai.

"We decide which route is the best to come and go from the house and disable one camera to give ourselves an exit point. We'll need to make sure we appear in front of the other cameras regularly. Make sure they think we're hanging around the house."

"Plan," Dillon said. "Ella, you're with me at all times. Don't sneak off to get some me-time."

Nikolai rolled his eyes, but his brother-in-law didn't understand how the guilt at Hana's death sat on his shoulders, heavy as a pack filled with a week's rations.

"Ella? I want your promise. These dudes aren't playing tiddlywinks."

That one earned him a guffaw from Nikolai and a grin from Ella. Making people laugh—that was more Josh than him. He felt his own lips quirk, and suddenly, they were all chuckling.

Dillon's sat-phone rang. "Williams."

"Dillon, the cops want to talk to you. I'm handing over the phone to Connor."

"Your sister has explained everything and given us the evidence. You think we should wait a few days until we execute a search warrant. Is that correct?"

"Yeah. We've found cameras on my property. They're keeping track of where I am and what I've been doing. They've watched me poking around and realized Hana was nosing into their affairs. That's why she's dead."

"You will not take things into your own hands." A statement.

Dillon opted for honesty. "I want to, but my brother-in-law and I discussed this and decided it was better to call you. They'll have advance warning if you travel in by vehicle. And I'm not sure what's going on with the neighbors on the other side. Maybe nothing since they're not as close as I am."

"Your sister said you're both SAS. Generally, I'd prefer civilians to stay away from an operation, but we could do with help," Connor said. "I'd like to hear your plan."

"The sheds where they store the birds are empty at present. The helicopter came two days ago, and we're guessing they took delivery of the birds on hand. We're assuming they're selling the birds on the dark web."

"What sort of birds are we talking about?" Connor said. "Which species have you spotted in the traps?"

"One was a kokako and another was a greenish parrot. No idea of the variety."

"A kaka?"

"No, I've seen flocks of kaka perched in the trees. They don't venture near the traps. One trap held a wood pigeon."

"I've spoken with my superiors, and we agree to wait for at least two days. Stay away from your neighbor and let him get on with his bird trapping."

"What if he gets another shipment of birds away?" Dillon asked.

"We'll be watching," Connor said in a hard, determined voice. "They will not get away from us this time."

·♥·♥·♥·♥·♥·

Tension vibrated in the room, in the air, until Ella wanted to scream. She'd spent the afternoon inside, boredom and uneasiness driving her to cook and clean. The same apprehension beset the two men, and they filled their afternoon by fixing the fence around the barn and scrutinizing the alpacas.

Now, darkness had fallen.

"The roast meat scent is making my belly rumble," Nikolai said. "Nose heaven."

Ella hid a smile. "Thank you."

Dillon prowled back and forth instead of taking a seat at the dinner table. "My gut is twitchy."

"Mine too," Nikolai agreed.

"You suspect they'll come here. Tonight?" Ella asked.

"It's a strong possibility. If not tonight, tomorrow," Dillon said with confidence. "They failed to grab you last night. They'll come again."

Ella's forehead scrunched. "But why do they want me?"

"Because Dillon has pissed them off," Nikolai said. "They want to send him a warning."

"Which they did when they barged into your house uninvited." Dillon swiped his hand through his hair. "Summer shouldn't have brought you here."

"I could have left with your sister," Ella snapped.

Nikolai shot a wide grin at Dillon. "He's made himself responsible for your safety. He likes you."

Dillon loosed a curse and sprang at Nikolai.

Nikolai darted out of his way, his hands raised in a surrender position. "Payback, mate. Payback."

Dillon released a snarl, and Ella decided that was enough. She stood and crossed the kitchen to get to Dillon. She placed her hands on his shoulders and waited until his attention centered on her. "Let's make a plan. You guys are excellent at using your brains to save people."

Nikolai's amusement dropped away. "Ella is right. An early warning system—that's what we need. Doesn't need to be fancy. A trip wire of some description that makes a din when they blunder into it."

"Good," Ella said, turning her full attention back to Dillon. "What else? You guys scheme while I serve dinner." She pulled two cans of beer out of the fridge and handed one to each man before she returned to her pot of beef curry. By the time she drained the rice, Nikolai and Dillon sat at the table and debated stringing wires versus rope and almost empty paint cans.

Ella served the curry and carried over two plates with man-size servings. She returned to the counter for her dinner and claimed the seat next to Dillon. "Do we have a plan? Will we have time to get ready if they come tonight?"

"We do," Nikolai confirmed.

"Can I help?"

Dillon cast her a searching glance before nodding. "You can."

"What about the cameras they've put up to watch you?" Ella asked. "Will that be a problem?"

"If I were them, I'd watch to make certain we were inside. They'd assume they were safe at night," Nikolai said.

"And not watching the camera recordings," Dillon concurred. "We'll set our traps as soon as we've finished eating. Let's put one camera out of commission to give ourselves an easy way out of the house. Great curry, Ella. Thank you for cooking dinner."

"I second that," Nikolai said and pushed away his empty plate. "Are there seconds?"

Ella gestured toward the pots on the cooktop. "Help yourself."

Arranging the tripwires, or ropes in this case since the materials on hand restricted them, fascinated her. She carted ropes and cans back and forth, watching and taking mental notes as the men assembled the crude alarm system. A man entering the property stealthily would miss the rope at ankle height.

"That should do it. I'm going to take a shower. Coming, Ella?" Dillon held out his hand to her.

Without a second thought, she placed her fingers in his.

"We'll see you in the morning, earlier if we have visitors," Dillon said to Nikolai.

"What about the dishes?" Ella asked.

"I'll do them," Nikolai said. "You cooked dinner."

Dillon tugged on her hand and she followed him to the bathroom. "Strip."

Ella blinked at him.

"Please. I'd like to shower with you." He turned on the water and rapidly disrobed.

When she dawdled, he helped her by unbuttoning her red shirt.

"This shirt was an inspired choice." He grinned, a beam wide enough to make a comedian proud. "Bright red like a matador's cape. No way they would've missed your presence."

"I wore it because it's my favorite shirt. I needed a confidence booster today." She shimmied out of her vintage-inspired jeans and pulled off her socks at the same time.

"Hana warned you?"

"Yes. If she hadn't..." She trailed off, a shudder working through her.

"You were smart hiding. It was the best plan. Otherwise, you might be dead. I couldn't stroke your luscious breasts again or suck your neck at the spot that makes you gasp." He followed words with action, and she did gasp. "I love your curves. So sexy and perfect for a man to grip while he's thrusting into your wet pussy."

His words thrilled her as much as his sensual caresses, but before she gave in to her coursing needs, she had a question. "Why were you grumpy with me today? I didn't—hadn't—done anything wrong."

Dillon sighed. "I'm sorry, sweetheart. I've already lost Hana and coming close to losing you as well..." He pressed his forehead to hers before nudging her under the warm water. "I'm trained as a soldier. It's my job to protect, and I've failed with both of you." He stepped into the shower and closed the door behind him.

"It's good I came to you," Ella said. "I can knock sense into that stubborn brain of yours." She tapped him on the side of the head. "I bet Hana loved you for giving her a new life."

Dillon swallowed, his throat working as his eyes closed. When his eyes opened again, grief filled them. "She loved me, but I couldn't return... I...I didn't feel the same way as her. It was clear she hoped our friendship might deepen. She told me not to worry, but her death..."

"Oh! I never realized. The local gossip... Your parents didn't know?"

"No," Dillon said.

"I'm sorry. That must've been difficult. For both of you." Her expression was shrewd as she studied him. "You're burdened with guilt because she died in what you thought was a safe place."

"How could I not be?"

"Hana was happy here. My gut tells me she was content. I bet she helped pick the colors for the rooms and set about making a home for both of you."

"She did."

"Hand me the soap."

Dillon offered her the soap and she turned him to rub it over his broad back. A citrus scent filled the shower as suds swirled down his spine and over his fine backside.

"Hana made me come here," Ella said. "She must have a purpose. She loved you, and although you didn't love her in the same way, she wants your happiness."

Dillon turned to face her. "Me and you? You like me?"

"Quite a bit, actually." This confession was a bad idea, but she preferred truth to evasion.

"I'm returning to Afghanistan soon."

"Yes, but that doesn't matter. Not right at this

moment."

He stared at her, his blue eyes dark and stormy and serious. "I have no words."

"No problem," she said, reaching up to kiss him.

In pure Dillon-style, he took over the kiss, his hands wandering her hips and breasts. Her arse. When her blood roared through her veins and desire drove her reactions, he pulled back.

"I want a soft bed." Regret pulled at his expression as he separated their bodies. "It's safer if we can listen for intruders."

And the shower impeded their hearing. She nodded and briskly washed while Dillon did the same. She stepped out of the shower and grabbed a towel to dry off.

"Don't bother getting dressed," Dillon said.

"But Nikolai—"

"Will shut his eyes if he wants to live."

"Do you like your brother-in-law?"

"Yes. Didn't at first. He grew on me like a rash."

"Charming."

Dillon slapped her backside. "Move. I'm about two seconds away from pouncing, and the condoms are two rooms away."

Ella peered from the bathroom and once she was certain Nikolai wasn't watching, she scuttled to Dillon's bedroom.

"Where is Nikolai sleeping?"

"Not with us." Dillon closed the door behind him. "He's big enough to look after himself." He scooped her off her feet and swung her onto the bed with easy strength. Seconds later, his big body covered hers, his mouth stopping further conversation.

Ella wrapped her arms around him and clung, determined to enjoy this private moment where everything was right between them. Dillon drove her onward, passion sweeping them under. Hands glided over her hips, parted her legs and lifted her to his mouth. A moan spilled free, and he grinned at her, his mouth shiny with her juices.

"Nikolai will hear."

Apparently comfortable with unintentional eavesdropping, he licked her again, doing precision work on her clit that had her crying aloud.

She bit her lip to stem her cries but failed, and Dillon chortled. The burst of air from his amusement had her on a knife edge of gratification. One final lick sent her tumbling over into pleasure. Sensation streaked to her toes. Dillon gentled his attentions before backing off, having already learned of her sensitivity after climax.

He moved up the bed, kissing her again. This time she tasted herself on his lips. Before she settled into the embrace, he pulled away.

"Condom," he said in a terse voice. "On your hands and knees."

She stared at him, slow to follow his instruction.

"Ella. Careful, I enjoy giving a good spanking. There is nothing prettier than a scarlet arse. It's the gift that keeps giving since the lingering soreness reminds the recipient of their man for the following days."

Ella swallowed while regarding his bright blue eyes. He'd

trimmed his beard again, and it suited him. "Are you my man?"

"I want to be, even though it's not smart. When I leave, I won't be back for at least six months." He ripped open the foil packet and rolled the latex onto his shaft.

Ella pulled her gaze away from his sexy, competent hands. Confidence and the trace of arrogance got her every time. Her gaze connected with his, and she noted the curve of his lips, the softer edge he normally kept hidden. "Are you telling me or warning me away?"

"Both. Hands and knees. Move fast, because the idea of punishing you is a temptation."

An imp in Ella told her to go slow since a spanking intrigued her and left her pussy pulsing with need, her nipples tight and aching. The increased curve of his lips and the glow in his blue eyes told her he'd read her mind with frightening ease.

"Hands and knees, Ella."

With a last survey of his broad chest and masculine determination, she flopped over onto her belly and slowly pushed into position. She'd scarcely settled when his hand cupped one buttock. His first smack startled an *oomph* from her. His second one a grunt, and the third smack had her crying out. He rubbed his hand over the stinging warmth of her buttock.

"In the interests of my sanity, I'm sticking to three tonight, because I didn't give you much of a warning. In the future, I expect you to follow my orders or I will spank you, and it will hurt you to sit because I won't stop at three swats. Is that clear?"

"Yes," Ella said in a low voice, unsure of how she felt about this new development. She'd ponder the matter later. The truth, Dillon's swats had left her pulse racing, her pussy wetter and her skin tingling with heat. Weirdly, the spanking had forged emotional ties. During the day, he was protective of those he cared for, and this new side of him had taken her by surprise.

"Stop thinking so hard." Dillon notched his cock to her and pushed inside until he could go no further.

"This information about you bears consideration. I had no idea. Why didn't you mention spanking earlier?"

"Because it's a private part of me, and I didn't know where we were going. We decided on friends with benefits. That's casual. Vanilla. Enough. We'll talk more tomorrow."

He tweaked her nipples until they stood erect and sensitive to his every tug. Only then did he withdraw and push back inside her. He set a fast pace, and one of his hands slid down to cup her mons. One finger unerringly stroked her clit, and her pussy rippled around his cock. His strokes became choppy after that but Ella was already hurtling toward another orgasm. She shattered, her loud cry bringing a flush to her cheeks. Dillon rocked into her and stilled, his groan a hoarse expulsion of air.

After a long moment, he separated their bodies and stood to deal with the condom. When he returned to the bed, he tugged her close and spooned. Ella relaxed, replete and safe in his arms. Dillon intrigued her with his many layers, and she could not wait to peel away more of his mysteriousness.

Dillon woke with a blast of cold air whistling against his back.

"They're coming."

Instantly, he shook Ella awake and placed his hand over her mouth until he was certain she wouldn't cry out and alert their visitors.

"Hana is here," he whispered. "She says they're coming. Get dressed and stay out of our way."

She nodded, and once she moved, he pulled on a pair of jeans and a T-shirt. He stuffed his feet in a pair of runners and hustled to wake Nikolai.

"Nikolai." He approached his brother-in-law carefully, fully aware of the danger in awakening a soldier.

"Yeah? No one has tripped our alarm."

"Hana says they're coming." Dillon muttered a curse when he realized what he'd said, but to his credit, Nikolai rose and pulled on his jeans.

"Dillon. Dillon. Dillon."

A harsh exclamation of air burst from Nikolai.

"Let's go," Dillon said.

Dillon opened the door and it swung wide without a squeak after they'd oiled the hinges earlier. He and Nikolai slipped outside and separated while they waited. Soon, low voices reached him. The two men were walking together instead of approaching separately from different directions. He glided into position, glad of the warning. He hadn't mentioned Hana to Nikolai because he hadn't been certain she'd make an appearance. But if his deceased wife had a yearning for revenge, he, for one, would go to her aid.

His pulse raced as he waited but he was confident of his abilities.

The first man blundered into their tripwire a few seconds ahead of the other. It was his signal to move, and he leaped on the nearest man, subduing him way too easily.

"Got him," Nikolai said from Dillon's right.

"We'll take them inside for questioning," Dillon said.

The man in his grip fought. He was as big as Dillon but had a soft belly and no endurance. The weapon—likely illegal—was no use to him if he had no access to it. The pair hadn't expected Dillon and Nikolai to be on guard, which showed a distinct lack of planning. Dillon shoved him through the door.

"What the hell, man? What are you doing?" Dillon's prisoner blustered and attempted to tear free of his grip again. Dillon recognized him as one of the men checking the traps, but other than that, he'd never met the big, burly blond. Without a word, he stripped off the man's jacket and did a visual for other weapons. He removed a knife and a radio before restraining the man with plastic cuffs on his wrists and a second set around his ankles.

Nikolai's captive took more subduing since he landed a punch on Nikolai's jaw. Nikolai cursed, but recovered rapidly. He used his legs to trip him and shoved him face-first into the floor. He, too, ripped off the guy's jacket and removed a knife before he cuffed him.

"Let us go," the blond demanded.

"Have you interrogated them?" Ella asked.

"I told you to stay in the bedroom." He'd already lost

one wife. Ella couldn't get hurt too. The acknowledgment had his thoughts stuttering for an instant before his brain fired to life again. From the first moment he'd spotted her, he'd sensed trouble.

"Should I call the cops?" she asked, his sat-phone in her hands.

"What the fuck! We have done nothing wrong," Nikolai's captive, a tall man with black hair. His body carried more muscle than the blond's. "You have no right to do this."

"No?" Ella said in a sweet voice. She stepped nearer, only stopping when Dillon growled.

Nikolai's brows rose and he wore a definite smirk. "If that's all you've got in the way of communication skills, it's no wonder you strike out with the ladies."

"Fuck off," Dillon snapped.

Ella ignored both of the soldiers. "You're sneaking around in the dark. You have a gun. You have a club thingie." She pointed at the short baton Nikolai had removed from the dark-haired man. "They're wearing the same footwear as the men who broke into my place. I'm calling the cops."

Dillon glanced at Nikolai and caught his brother-in-law's shrug. "Go ahead."

Before she finished dialing, the radio the blond had been carrying squawked. "Come in," a masculine voice demanded.

Dillon's brows rose in query and Nikolai nodded. "Yeah?" He kept it short and sweet, his voice gruff.

The blond shouted and before Dillon could move, Ella

grabbed a jacket and shoved it over his head, muffling his protests. Dillon strode from the lounge and headed for the bedroom.

"What was that?"

"Fucker tripped in the dark." Dillon waited.

"You done?"

"Yeah."

"Good. Clear the kiwi traps. We've got a white." Excitement and greedy gloating filled the man's voice.

Damn. He had no idea of the location of the traps. After a brief hesitation, he took a gamble. "Which trap?"

"The one by the stream, just inside the reserve. As soon as you bring the bird, I'll contact the buyer." He ended the call.

Dillon returned to the lounge to find that Nikolai had slapped gaffer tape over the men's mouths.

"What's happening?"

"By the sounds of it, they've trapped a white kiwi and the boss wants these guys to collect it before he contacts the buyer. Have you rung the cops?"

"They're on their way," Nikolai said. "Connor said to hang fire."

"A white kiwi?" Ella asked. "The bird sanctuary has one. They're incredibly rare. He could receive millions for it on the black market."

"I'll ring Connor back." Dillon dialed. "Connor, it's Dillon. A new development." He explained. "What do you want us to do?"

"Damn. If we delay too long, the guy will get suspicious."

"What if Nikolai and I put on these guys' jackets and go to retrieve the kiwi?" Dillon asked.

"The helicopter has arrived. Is there a spot to land at your place?"

"Yeah. We can mark it out with lights."

"Right. I'll send your two prisoners back in the helicopter with one of my guys. By the time we arrive, I'll have a plan worked out with the boss."

"See you soon." Dillon disconnected. "We need to mark out a spot for the chopper to land. They're on their way."

They used torches and tea lights sitting in his pots and pans. With the landing zone marked, he and Nikolai hauled a prisoner each out of his house. It didn't take long until the *whop-whop* of a helicopter approached his land.

"Ella, can you bag the gun and knives and other stuff we removed from these guys? The cops will want it. I have zip-lock bags in the pantry. Use a tea towel or something similar to pick them up."

Ella pursed her lips. "They have your prints on them."

"They don't need yours too."

The helicopter landed without difficulty. Connor and three other cops strode toward him. One cop returned to Eketahuna in the chopper with the prisoners while Connor and the other two remained.

"This is the plan," Connor said. "Dillon, you and I will retrieve the bird. We deliberated on releasing it but decided we need to keep the kiwi short-term for the evidence chain. We've contacted the experts at the sanctuary. They weren't aware of another white kiwi. Nikolai, I want you to guide my colleagues to the farm."

"The guy is paranoid. He has cameras everywhere," Dillon said. "He even has cameras on my property to keep track of my comings and goings."

"The man will be beside himself at trapping a white kiwi. He might not be too worried about keeping his eye on his security system. Besides, it's the daytime visits he'll be more worried about," Ella said.

"I agree," Dillon said. "He didn't realize he wasn't talking to his employee."

"What do we do when we get to the neighbor's place?" Nikolai asked.

"I'm betting he will contact us again, asking about the kiwi," Dillon said. "He'll be anxious."

Connor nodded. "Wait until you see us enter the neighbor's property with the bird before you move. We have a search warrant. We'll act on it then."

"What if he catches the reek of rat?" Nikolai asked.

Ella nodded. "Yeah, what if he destroys evidence?"

"I doubt he will because the birds are worth big money," Connor said.

"We need to move," Dillon said. "Here." He handed over the larger jacket to Connor. Dillon owned a jacket that resembled the second one.

Five minutes later, they were on their way.

Ella waited until Dillon disappeared before turning to Nikolai. "I'm coming with you. After what has happened tonight, I refuse to stay here on my own."

"Dillon won't be happy."

"Too bad," Ella said. "He's not here. I promise to stay

179

SHELLEY MUNRO

at the back of the line and follow orders. I'm used to tramping through the bush. I won't delay you."

"You will follow us, anyway," Nikolai guessed.

"Summer has trained you well." She offered a sweet smile when Nikolai growled, sounding much like Dillon. Must be a soldier thing.

"This is the deal. You walk at the back of our group. Do not slow us down. Follow every order."

Her brows rose. "And if I don't?"

"Dillon will spank you."

Heat gathered in Ella's cheeks, and it took long seconds for her to realize her mouth hung open. She snapped it shut. "You eavesdropped on us."

"It was difficult not to. Perhaps that's where I took a wrong turn with Summer," he mused to himself.

"You are not a gentleman."

"Just the way Summer likes me," Nikolai said cheerfully.

"I'll keep up," she snapped when she noticed the two cops listening to their conversation. "Let's go." She took two steps out of the front door before Nikolai's hand closed around her biceps.

"Cameras," he reminded her.

Ella's stomach sank and chastised, she nodded. She followed Nikolai and the other two cops—James and Grant, from memory—along the side of Dillon's house. A safe path to avoid the one still-functioning camera. Thankfully, Ella was fit and she'd donned her boots, but the men slunk along the path at a rapid clip. They didn't use torches, relying on the light of the moon and the approach of dawn.

180

It was darker under the trees, but Ella trotted after the men, telling herself she didn't have time to act the wuss. This was too important.

This man—Dillon's neighbor—mustn't get away with poaching New Zealand's native birds and a valuable and rare white kiwi.

12

A SEARCH FOR A WHITE KIWI

Dillon led Connor straight to the boundary fence, not bothering to take the time to disable cameras. With hats plopped on their heads and Connor wearing the confiscated jacket, their neighbor should assume his workers were on the way.

The workers' radio crackled. "What took you so long?"

Dillon shot a glance at Connor and kept walking. He depressed the talk button on the radio. "You try subduing two big dudes. Took time."

"I've contacted the buyer. He wants the kiwi even if it's old. Handle it carefully. Remember how I showed you?"

"Yeah," Dillon barked while wondering if the man was always this chatty and confiding with his employees. Unless the workers got a cut of the profits. It would keep the men keen and stop their tongues from wagging. Something to mention later although the cops were probably already checking their backgrounds and financials.

He and Connor leaped over the fence and slid into the sanctuary land.

"Not that turn," the voice on the radio crackled. "What is wrong with you? Next one on the right."

Dillon and Connor backtracked and took the turning,

"It's the first trap," the voice said over the radio.

Dillon scowled at the undergrowth. Where the hell was the camera? They needed it off so they could bumble around in privacy.

The radio crackled. "Where are you going?"

"He's taking a leak."

"Not in front of the bloody camera," the man snapped as Connor slipped into the undergrowth. The cop paused, the sound of his fly zipper loud in the early morning.

"Not there. I don't wanna record your cock."

Dillon bit back a triumphant grin. At least they'd discovered the location of the camera.

"Crap!" the voice came over the radio. "The helicopter has come early. I'll meet the pilot. Hurry and bring the kiwi. Don't fuck this up."

Dillon paused a beat.

"Got it," Connor said in a low voice.

"Will that be our side?"

"Hopefully," Connor muttered glancing at the trees. "Although they've gone in early. Got it." He clambered up an old manuka tree. "It's off."

"Let's find this kiwi." Dillon hesitated, his heart overruling his head for once. He wasn't sure how Connor would take his suggestion. "Connor, I understand you guys want evidence, but it would be less stressful for the bird if we let it go in its own territory. Could we take photos instead?"

Connor scrambled downward a fraction and jumped the rest of the way to the ground. "That's what I was thinking. We have two workers under arrest. We've got Hana's photos, and we'll have footage from Reese Markham's property. I've got my phone." Connor snapped a photo of the disarmed camera.

After noting the direction the camera pointed, they separated to search for the trapped kiwi.

"It's here," Dillon said, indicating a fallen tree. He stood aside while Connor took photos. "Once the details get out to the public everyone will be searching for this kiwi."

"Yeah, I'm not sure how to get around that."

"Ella might have suggestions since she works at the sanctuary."

"I'll give the director a call once we're done here." Connor squatted to take a photo of the white kiwi.

With the approaching day, the bird had huddled in a ball, and it reminded Dillon of the white hat his grandmother used to wear to christenings and weddings when he was a kid.

"I have enough photos for evidence," Connor said. "You can let it out of the trap."

Dillon propped open the door and stood out of the way. When nothing happened, he moved behind the trap. The kiwi unfurled and shot out of the confined area. Dillon got a glimpse of furry white feathers, strong claws and a black beak before the bird scuttled into a clump of green ferns and disappeared.

"Did you get a photo?" Dillon demanded. "Ella will be interested."

Connor tapped on his phone. "I did." The pleasure faded from his face. "Let's get this bastard. Show me the way to Reese's farm."

Dillon led the way through the bush, going faster than they had because they didn't need to dodge cameras or step carefully because of the dark.

When the farm came into view, a police helicopter stood near the big silver barn and uniformed policemen swarmed through the yard.

"Did you get him?" Connor demanded of the first uniform they neared.

"We did." Satisfaction rang in the policewoman's tone. "They've already arrested him and flown him out."

Dillon spotted Nikolai and headed in that direction. A curse exploded from his mouth when Ella appeared beside him, distinctive with her pink hair.

"What are you doing here?" He didn't give her a chance to reply, turning to Nikolai with anger surging through his body. "Why did you bring her here?"

"She threatened to follow on her own. I figured it was safer if I could keep an eye on her." Nikolai glanced at Dillon. "I warned her you'd spank her for disobedience."

Dillon eyed Ella. He raised his brows and color seeped into her cheeks before she shifted her focus from him. Point made. He turned back to Nikolai. "Is this guy responsible for Hana's death?"

"No one has mentioned that. They're too busy photographing the scene and collecting evidence. There are a few birds in the shed."

"Native?"

"Yes."

"Is it safe for me to peek?" Ella asked. "What happened to the kiwi?"

Dillon lowered his voice. "We decided it was better to let it go. Less stress for the bird and it could return to its own territory."

"Good. That's good. Was it truly a white one?"

"Yeah, Connor took photos. He said he'd send them to you."

"Wow! We thought Manukura was the only white kiwi. Everyone at work will be excited." She cocked her head and studied the cages. "I wonder if Connor will let me release these birds?"

Dillon placed a hand on her shoulder and pulled her against his side. "Let's ask him."

Half an hour later, after Connor and his team had photographed the contents of the shed and the different birds, he, Ella, Connor, and Nikolai carried a bird cage each. Dillon toted a pair of kokako with their distinctive bright blue wattles while Ella had a kaka, the ear-piercing shrieks of the parrot informing everyone he'd had enough of captivity.

"The birds are healthy enough. At least they cared for them," Ella said, her gaze darting from cage to cage. "I don't know how they caught the riflemen. They're so tiny and shy."

"Ella, will this be far enough away from the buildings?" Connor asked.

"Let's walk as far as those trees." She pointed to the group of four trees ahead of them.

"You first, Ella," Dillon said. "Your kaka is giving me a headache."

"And if you keep glaring like that, we'll suspect Ella is giving you a headache," Nikolai said.

Dillon bit his tongue, aware that he deserved every one of Nikolai's comments since he and Josh had given Nikolai such a hard time when he'd hooked up with Summer. In truth, they'd given their sister headaches before she'd left Eketahuna for the big bad of Auckland. Summer had grown a backbone to thwart them and decided on Nikolai, who was a decent bloke. Nikolai treated Summer well, and their love and respect showed in their intimate smiles and surreptitious caresses. That earned his brother-in-law a pass.

Ella set down the cage and opened the door. The parrot hopped toward the open gap and peered out. He strutted from the cage, flapped his wings and took off. Dillon caught the flash of scarlet beneath the bird's green wings before the parrot disappeared over the hill.

They released the other birds, one cage at a time. The tiny riflemen headed straight for the branches of the closest trees while the kokako followed the path of the kaka. The pigeon, or kereru, took off with a laborious flap of wings. For an instant Dillon wondered if the bird would make it, such was the effort it expended. But finally, the heavy bird flew toward the reserve, the *whop-whop-whop* of its wings audible long after it disappeared from sight.

"Do you need us for anything else?" Nikolai asked Connor. "Statements or anything like that?"

"We will be busy here for a while," Connor said. "Why don't you come to the police station tomorrow morning? We'll take your statements then."

Dillon nodded agreement. "We'll be there."

"Summer will be glad to cuddle me," Nikolai said. "I'll get to sleep in a bed tonight with my sexy wife instead of on your uncomfortable couch."

Dillon ignored him and turned to Ella. "You can go home now. The guys that broke into your place are in custody."

Ella blinked once. "All right. I'm due back at work the day after tomorrow. I take it we're walking? Shall we go?" She strode off and powered up the hill with long strides.

Nikolai cuffed him over the head. "Numskull."

"What? What did you do that for?"

"Ella likes you. I have no idea why, but she does. Ask her to stay with you."

"I'm heading back to Afghanistan. They contacted me this morning and told me they want me back."

"Why didn't you say anything?"

"I'm telling you now." Dillon followed Ella, and Nikolai fell into step with him. "It will be at least six months before I'm home in New Zealand again. Anything could happen."

"Did you talk to Ella about it? Ask her what she wanted to do?"

"No."

"Fool." Nikolai shot him a look. "Women like us to ask for their opinions. Something I've learned from your sister."

"Not talking about it," Dillon snapped. "Ring Summer and tell her to meet you and Ella at the road. I'll give you a lift there."

Of all the stupid, pigheaded men. Ella stomped up the hill, fast enough to make her muscles burn. She'd presumed he'd wanted her with him, that she'd made progress and they sat on the same page. A mistake on her part.

Idiot.

She wouldn't make the same one again.

If Dillon Williams didn't want her in his life. *Fine.* She'd move on without the angst and complications that came with the grumpy man.

Ella reached the hill summit and took the most direct route to Dillon's house. The sooner she packed her bag and left, the faster she could reach the haven of her home. Then, and only then, she could shout and scream and stick pins in a Dillon-type figure.

And if the ghost made an appearance—Hana—Ella would direct her to Dillon because she was done with this. From what Connor had told her when she'd had a quick word, it sounded as if they'd helped to catch the people responsible for Hana's murder. Didn't that mean Hana could move on to wherever ghosts hung out once they'd settled their affairs?

Whatever.

She was done.

13

DILLON MAKES A MISTAKE

ELLA HADN'T SPOKEN TO him since they'd left the neighbor's place. Dillon shot her a side glance and noticed her set features, her tight jaw. Her don't-mess-with-me vibe.

He let out a sigh, every part of him wanting to go to her. He didn't.

Not wise, for one. Soon he'd be back in the thick of war.

It wasn't fair to expect Ella to wait for him. So many contingencies he couldn't control.

"Are you sure this is how you want things to end?" Nikolai asked in a low voice. "I was an idiot with your sister. It took me ages to realize it was better for us to be together than apart. And it pissed me off when she dated someone else. You don't want that Dillon. Your expression when you watch the woman gives you away. Last night didn't sound like a couple who should separate."

"Butt out," Dillon said with a growl. "It's none of your business."

Nikolai raised his hands in surrender. "Don't mind me. When are you flying out to Afghanistan?"

"Wednesday," Dillon said. "My cover injured himself during a night recon."

Nikolai nodded, but Dillon could tell he had a lot more to say. To his credit, he took Dillon's warning to heart and didn't verbalize more of his opinion. With an uncertain future, it was best if Ella moved on without him. The dart of pain to his chest, the echo in his mind took him by surprise. A grunt emerged, earning a questioning glance from Nikolai. Dillon ignored the silent offer to listen to whatever was going through his head. Instead, he kept walking.

When they arrived back at Dillon's house, Ella stomped to his bedroom. The thumps and bangs hinted at her temper. Guilt made Dillon steer clear. This woman—this spitfire of a woman with her pink hair and attitude had gotten to him and that silent acknowledgement upped his remorse. Upped his irritation.

"I've called Summer. She's coming to collect us in half an hour," Nikolai said. "You coming with us?"

Dillon shook his head. "I need to do a few things before I take off on Wednesday. When are you and Summer flying back to Auckland?"

"Monday afternoon."

"I'll come and visit before you leave. I have to speak with Dad about looking after Rufus and my alpacas, anyway. Connor wants to take our statements tomorrow

191

morning."

"I'm ready." Ella lifted her chin in a sassy show of defiance.

Dillon watched her, taking in everything and committing it to memory. Her pink hair. Her curvy figure. Yes, it was the right thing to do—let her go—but it still hurt like a bitch. Much more than he expected, given their short acquaintance.

Dillon gave Nikolai and Ella a lift to the landslide.

Nikolai lifted his hand in farewell. "Catch you tomorrow."

Ella walked away without another word. Sorrow sliced through Dillon's gut yet again as he drove back to his house. Sex always fucked up everything.

· ❤ · ❤ · ❤ · ❤ · ❤ ·

ELLA TOSSED AND TURNED until the bedcovers twisted into impossible knots. Finally, she flopped onto her back and stared at the ceiling. She'd wondered if nerves and fear might hit after the break-in but the emotion that roiled through her reeked of anger. Bloody Dillon Williams. That bearded, bad-tempered behemoth had crept into her heart. He'd stolen it the second she'd let down her guard.

The louse.

At least something good had come from this debacle. They'd helped to stop a poaching ring and it looked as if they might've discovered the truth about Hana's death. Silver linings. The sex had been good. A break in a dry spell was never a bad move. Yep. *Silver linings.*

"Ella. Ella. Ella."

The air took on an icy coolness that pebbled goose bumps across her arms.

"Go away," Ella snapped and closed her eyes.

"Ella."

This time the voice sounded the same but different. Different enough to arouse her curiosity.

A petite woman with long, loose black hair stood in the middle of her bedroom. She wore jeans, a pink T-shirt and a denim jacket embroidered with pink roses. A pair of stout boots completed her outfit. Somehow, despite the darkness in her bedroom, Ella spotted her without difficulty. She'd been a stunning woman. One perfect for Dillon.

"Hana?" Ella croaked.

The woman smiled. "Yes."

"Why are you here? Those were the men who killed you."

"Yes." Hana lost her smile. "They intended to scare me. That's all. I remember falling. I must've hit my head."

"Doesn't matter if it was an accident or not. They should've come forward and confessed."

"They were frightened. Please tell Connor."

"I will." Ella frowned and sat. She propped her pillows against the headboard for comfort. "What happens now? To you, I mean."

Hana frowned. "I haven't finished here. You and Dillon—"

"Stop right there," Ella snapped. "There is no Dillon for me. He's an arrogant, bossy jerk, and I don't want him in my life. Go away. Bother Dillon and leave me out of this. He's leaving soon. Returning to Afghanistan."

"I thought... The two of you are perfect for each other. He radiates happiness when he spends time with you. You give him something I couldn't." Hana frowned and faded until she was no longer visible.

The chilliness lifted from her bedroom. Ella rearranged her pillows and closed her eyes. Perhaps now she could sleep.

·♥·♥·♥·♥·♥·

DILLON ARRIVED AT HIS parents' place not long after seven and before it was fully light. His mother was in the kitchen and the scent of pancakes filled the air. He took a seat at the kitchen table where he'd eaten meals as a child.

"You walked? Why didn't you ring? Steven could've met you."

Dillon shrugged. "It didn't take long." The truth, it had given him time to decide he'd made the right decision. Hana had died because he hadn't been there for her. Ella had almost died too because of the poaching mess. It was much better if he returned to Afghanistan and did his job. Let Ella move on. Hana too.

"Nikolai said you're returning to Afghanistan."

His mother was watching him with an eagle eye—the one she'd used when they were kids and suspected they'd been up to mischief. Mostly she'd been right, but not this time.

"Yeah."

"You'll want us to look after your stock."

"If you can. If not, I'll arrange for someone else to take care of them. It's not as easy with the blocked road."

"We'll do it. Gives your father something to do. The warmer weather will arrive soon. We'll bring Rufus home and check on your alpacas every second day. Cliff will be happy to help if we need to go away for some reason."

"Thanks, Mum."

"You're welcome. Summer said there was something between you and Ella."

Dillon waited for a beat while he dealt with his temper. "Summer has a big mouth, and in this case, she has no idea what she's talking about. Ella is a nice girl. We're friends. That's all."

His mother pulled a face. "Nice. Oh, dear."

Dillon took the less is more approach. Always better with his mother. He shrugged. "We're expected at the police station to give a statement."

"Nikolai and Summer told us. A terrible business. Poor Hana. At least, we have a better idea of what happened to her and why. Are you sure you need to go back to Afghanistan? I know you miss Hana. I—"

And there went his mother again. "Mum, someone needs to keep an eye on Josh. Besides, I signed up for this."

A harsh sigh rippled from his mother. "I worry," she said simply. "One son is bad enough but two plus a son-in-law in the same business."

Dillon grinned. Only his mother could reduce war to a work-like matter. "What's for breakfast? Can I do anything to help?"

"Set the table for me."

Dillon stood and made quick work of the task he'd undertaken since he was five. Nikolai and Summer arrived, his brother-in-law cradling their son. His father appeared carrying two bottles of milk and the newspaper.

"Ah, a full house," he said. "I understand you have to report to the police station this morning."

Talk turned to the poaching.

"Rumors are already floating around the town," his father said. "I never added to them, but the speculation made for interesting eavesdropping."

"We suspect the poaching has been going on for a while," Summer said.

"It pisses me off that it was happening under my nose," Dillon said.

"I should've noticed something," his father said. "I didn't. Neither did the cops who investigated Hana's murder."

"Hopefully, we'll learn more soon. I hated suspecting someone in the district might've been responsible for Hana's death. I loved that girl," his mother said. "I'd hoped for more grandchildren."

"Make do with one grandson," Dillon said in a firm voice. "You want more, you guilt Summer and Nikolai." He almost laughed at the expressions on Summer's and Nikolai's faces. His humor died a fast death when he spotted Hana standing in the kitchen. She wore faded jeans, a Groot T-shirt and her favorite denim jacket.

"*Brrrr!* It's chilly all of a sudden," his mother said.

Dillon continued to gape at Hana.

"Something wrong, Dillon?" Summer stared at him.

"No." Dillon hid his shock with his coffee mug. Did none of them see her?

Hana stalked toward him, confident in a way she'd never been during their time together in Afghanistan. She met his gaze and smiled as if she could read his mind.

"We will talk." It was Hana's firm no-nonsense voice, the one she used when she dealt with those she considered idiots.

"Go ahead," Dillon said.

"Go ahead with what," his mother said.

Dillon glanced away from Hana's cheeky grin to his family. Their reactions varied from curious to thoughtful.

None of them acknowledged Hana's presence. Although he was sure Nikolai had sensed her the night the intruders had come to his house. Not this time though.

"They're not aware of me," Hana said. "Just you and Ella see me. The others sense my presence. Don't know why so don't bother asking."

Dillon narrowed his eyes.

"Dillon?" his mother prompted. "What is wrong?"

"Nothing," he said.

Nikolai's snort told Dillon his brother-in-law believed otherwise. Too bad.

Dillon stood to refill his coffee mug. "Anyone else want coffee?" On receiving assents, he did the rounds with the coffeepot and the milk jug.

"Ella is perfect for you," Hana said. "She isn't a mouse, but she likes it when you spank her."

Dillon froze, only snapping out of it when his mother

shrieked because he'd overfilled her mug with milk. "Sorry." He grabbed a cloth to mop the spill while Hana giggled.

The musical joy had him freezing again. Had she ever acted this carefree?

"Dillon!" The stern tone told Dillon it wasn't the first time his mother had said his name. "What is wrong with you today? I hope you don't behave like this in Afghanistan. That is not a safe place for daydreamers."

Hana let out another peal of laughter, and frustration filled him because if he started a conversation with her, his family would accuse him of losing the plot.

"You've hurt Ella," Hana said. "Idiot. You were honest from the start, telling me you didn't love me. Stupidly, I told myself I could change your mind. I get it now. We were better as friends. But I don't understand why you're walking away from Ella and the happiness you could have together."

"She almost died," Dillon said, his tone harsh because the idea of a world without Ella in it hurt.

"Dillon?" Distinct worry etched into his mother's features.

Dillon huffed out a breath. "Do you want help with the dishes?"

"No," Summer said.

"Dad, can you look after Rufus and the alpacas? Mum said it was okay, but you're the one doing the work."

"Happy to do it, son. You need not worry about anything. If I have any problems, I'll email you."

"Dillon, why are you pushing Ella away when she is the

best thing that has ever happened to you?" Hana asked.

This time, Dillon held his tongue.

"If you don't require our help to clean, Dillon and I will head to the police station," Nikolai said.

Dillon gave a curt nod. Hana continued her determined chatter. What was wrong with Ella? She was nice. She was beautiful. She enjoyed sex with him. Dillon tasted blood by the time he slid into the passenger seat. His breath eased out as he clicked the seatbelt into place.

"You don't get away from me that easily," Hana said. "I'll follow you to Afghanistan if I have to convince you to give Ella a chance."

"Did she put you up to this?" Dillon snapped.

"Of course not," Hana replied. "I like her. She'll find another man, and you'll be sorry."

"She is better off with another man."

Nikolai backed out of the driveway and headed to the police station. "You're not the type to talk to yourself."

"Hana is sitting in the back seat."

"You haven't drunk anything stronger than coffee."

"You sensed something the other night even though you said nothing."

Nikolai frowned and slowed as they entered the town zone. "I told myself I was imagining things. Hana is in the rear?"

"Yep."

"How long has she been hanging around you?"

"This is the first time I've observed her. Before this, she yammered nonstop."

"Can she tell you what happened to her?"

"We hadn't got that far. She's been busy trying to poke her nose into my personal affairs," Dillon said. "Hana?"

"They caught me taking photos. I'd noticed the traps and had worked out what was going on. I'd intended going to the police, but I waited to take photos for proof."

Dillon repeated this back to Nikolai.

"They came to the house and demanded I hand over my camera. I don't think they expected me to fight. One of them pushed me and I fell. I remember the pain as I hit my head, and that's the last thing I recall."

"It sounds as if her death was an accident," Dillon told Nikolai. "She fell and hit her head."

"And they panicked," Nikolai guessed. "Why didn't they take her camera?"

"I had two cameras," Hana said. "One was in the craft room and the other in the kitchen. It had pictures of birds on it. They assumed they were in the clear."

Dillon explained this.

"Does Hana think you're making a mistake with Ella?"

"Yes. Yes!" Hana said and patted Nikolai on the shoulder in approval.

"Fuck!" The car drifted over the median line before Nikolai corrected his steering. "She really is here."

"I'm not making this up," Dillon said his tone cold. "My imagination isn't that good."

"He is walking away from something good with Ella," Nikolai announced.

"Thank you very much." Sarcasm trembled in Dillon's words. The instant the car pulled into a park outside the police station and came to a halt, he exited.

"You are making a mistake," Hana said.

Dillon rolled his eyes. "You weren't such a pain in the arse before."

"Things are different in New Zealand. I gained confidence. I liked it here, Dillon. So much. I was happy. You gave me that, and I never got the chance to thank you."

"I'm glad you were happy." Dillon noticed Nikolai was looking from him to the right. He resembled a person watching a tennis match. He could have told him that Hana stood in front of him, her hands placed on her jeans-clad hips.

"I'd be happier if you were settled. You're restless. Lonely. Or at least you were before I sent Ella to you. Since you met her, you've been happier. You've taken care of your appearance."

Hana's words brought a wash of regret and that damn guilt again.

"What do you suggest?" he asked, his voice gruff with emotions he hated to name.

"Go to her. Apologize. Ask her if she's willing to wait for you. You can communicate by email and phone while you're away. Get to understand each other." Hana bounced up and down on her toes in her enthusiasm.

"You've thought about this."

"Apart from helping to stop your neighbor, I didn't have much else to do."

"Better get this done," Nikolai said.

"Ella's coming," Hana said, and she blinked out of sight.

A bicycle appeared, and Dillon took a moment to watch Ella before she noticed him and Nikolai. Her pink hair fluttered in the breeze as she cycled.

"Have you just arrived?" She swung her leg over to dismount and leaned the bike against the brick wall of the police station.

"Yes," Nikolai said when it became obvious Dillon was too busy gawking to reply.

Before Dillon could second guess himself, he said, "Ella, could I talk to you in private once we're finished here? We could grab a coffee or something."

She sent him a searching glance. "Okay."

"Yes. Yes. Yes!"

The jubilant voice came from above them and both he and Ella lifted their heads.

"This is not our imagination," Ella said.

"Unfortunately. Hana has turned pushy since she arrived in New Zealand," Dillon said.

"It's called character growth," Hana shouted.

The door to the police station opened to reveal Connor. "Are you coming inside or not? I don't have all day."

The statements didn't take long. They kept to the facts—apart from announcing Hana's presence—and told the truth.

"What will happen next?" Ella asked.

"We've already formally charged them. Despite their lawyer's assertions, the judge decided they're a flight risk and we're holding them. The two lackeys have confessed to being at your place when Hana died. They say Hana fell hard and smacked her head on the hearth."

Dillon nodded. "Plausible scenario. Hana owned two cameras and they thought they'd grabbed all the photos.

They missed the camera sitting in Hana's craft room, which is the one we found."

"What about the birds they sold?" Nikolai asked.

"Most of them have gone overseas. The helicopter dropped them on a boat. Unfortunately, it's unlikely we'll recover them, but we'll contact the overseas authorities. We might catch the rest of our thieves yet. If it wasn't for you, no one would've noticed the poaching. The Mt. Bruce sanctuary conducts counts but they wait until the spring."

"Is that all you need from us, Connor?" Dillon asked. "I'm heading back to join my team, and I have things to arrange before I leave on Wednesday."

Connor frowned. "We'll need you to testify during the court case. I'll speak to my boss. Given the circumstances, they might approve you testifying via video conference."

Dillon offered a curt nod and turned to Ella. "Should we have that coffee now?"

She lifted her chin and met his steady gaze with a glare. "If you insist."

Nikolai sniggered, much in the way his brother Josh would've if he'd been present. Dillon ignored the interruption. He opened the door for Ella, waited for her to exit before scooting through himself and letting the door shut in Nikolai's face. Nikolai's guffaw made it through the barrier.

Hana walked right through the door. "That was childish, Dillon."

"What are you? My mother?"

"I was your wife." Sorrow filled her dark eyes for an

instant. "I liked being married to you, but it's time for you to move on. Leave your guilt behind."

"I don't—"

Hana flapped her hand in dismissal. "Don't try fibbing to me. I miss nothing."

Beside him, Ella gasped. "You saw everything?"

Dillon narrowed his eyes at Hana, and after a long pause, she chortled.

"I stayed out of the bedroom," Hana said when she could speak again. "But I saw the kissing. It made me envious." Then, she shrugged. "I have no regrets. Our marriage gave me freedom and happiness. I made friends here and felt useful. Living in our house and tending our animals, the ability to do what I wanted when I wanted was pure joy for me. Never say you've failed me, Dillon, because you offered me a life where people liked and respected me. You gave me a family who I adored, and best of all, I had your friendship. Yes, I wanted more. I wouldn't be human if I didn't, but I was content and few people from my country can say that."

A lump formed in Dillon's throat and he had to cough to clear the blockage. His first impulse was to deny Hana's words, but the delay let his beleaguered brain catch up. "Thanks. I valued your friendship and everything you did for me and my friends in Afghanistan."

"It was my pleasure." An expression of pure joy shone on Hana's face. "Remember me now and then, Dillon Williams. Ella, please look after him for me. He acts big and tough, but he's sometimes a little slow." She tapped her temple and winked. "I love you, Dillon. Make me proud."

Slowly, Hana's form faded. A joyful laugh drifted on the air for an instant before silence fell.

Dillon cleared his throat. "Would you like to go for coffee now? Please."

Ella stared at him for a long moment before her shoulders relaxed. "Now is fine."

Nerves struck Dillon as he walked at her side. They danced in the pit of his gut and sent darts of doubt to assail his mind.

What if Hana was wrong? What if all Ella had wanted was a soldier lover to brag about to her friends? There were women like that. He'd met a few in his time. As he always did in times of stress, he centered his breathing and took deep, measured inhalations. No. If anything, Ella was angry at him. If she'd wanted to bag a soldier, nothing he did would upset her. She'd move on without a glance over her shoulder.

"This is my favorite cafe," Ella said, coming to a halt in front of the Jumpy Rabbit.

Dillon opened the door. "What do you want to drink?"

"I'll have a trim latte, please. I'll grab a table."

Dillon acknowledged her suggestion and strode to the short line at the register. He placed their order—a latte with skim milk for Ella and a long black for him. On spying the cheese scones, still hot from the oven, he ordered two.

"Here are your scones and your number," the cashier chirped, her blonde ponytail bopping with every nod of her head. "We'll deliver the coffee to your table."

"Thank you." Dillon strode between the tables to reach

the one Ella had chosen against the wall. At least half of the dozen tables were empty, but the line at the counter had increased. They directed most of the gazes at him and each bore nosy curiosity. He pulled out a seat and sat. "Why is everyone staring?"

Amusement scooted across Ella's expressive face, her nose wrinkling for an instant. "Your mother talks about you and your brother, and locals regard you as heroes."

"But we're doing our job."

Ella shrugged. "And now you have helped to catch and stop a poaching ring. That's huge. I bet it will make tonight's news."

Dillon scowled. "Hell! I hope not. I'm meant to stay in the background. It's much better for my health and for those in my team."

"You should mention that to Connor."

Dillon called Connor and had a short conversation. The cop assured him he'd considered that and their official statement had not revealed their names. Once Dillon completed the call, he placed his phone on the table.

"Hana cared about you."

"Yes." Her death might have been an accident, but regret filled him anew. Sometimes life wasn't fair to good people. "I'm sorry I was abrupt with you yesterday. It's just my future is uncertain, and I didn't want you to wait for me. To put your life on hold." He held her gaze for as long as he could before glancing away. He stared at the back of his hand where he rested it on the tabletop.

Strong fingers gripped his hand. They squeezed until he lifted his head to meet her hard stare.

"Isn't that my decision? I'm an adult. I should get an equal say in our future."

"We haven't—"

"Here is your coffee," the waitress chirped.

"Thank you, Anne-Marie," Ella said in polite dismissal.

She continued to dally, her avid curiosity a palpable thing. "Let me know if I can bring you anything else." When they added nothing, she let out a huff and flounced back to her position behind the counter.

"The locals are also wondering about you and me," Ella said in an even voice that gave him no clue as to her stand on them as a couple.

Perhaps he should lay everything out and let her make the final decision. Yeah. That was what Nikolai had suggested, and he'd learned from his mother and his sister that women preferred to have their say.

"I like you a lot. I've enjoyed spending time with you, but I'm heading back to a war zone. I might not return home. You... Me..." He swallowed. "I hate that you'd need to wait. Put your life on hold for me."

"Pffff!" Ella said, startling him and the group of ladies sitting nearest to their table. She winked as the four ladies leaned closer, craning their necks to better eavesdrop on their private conversation. "I've dated since arriving in Eketahuna, but until you, I hadn't slept with any man. Does that tell you anything?"

"That you're careful and you don't sleep around."

"Exactly! I like you too, Dillon Williams, and it won't be putting my life on hold while I'm waiting for you to come home. I'll do what I've always done. Go out with my friends. Work at Mt. Bruce. Enjoy my hobbies. I might attend Zumba and line dancing for a start. Practice my spinning. Don't worry. I'll keep busy."

"What about sex?" Dillon asked.

"If I get desperate, I'll get out my vibrator or I might engage in phone sex occasionally with you."

Tension bled from Dillon. Above all, he trusted Ella. The woman had integrity. This might work if they both tried. "We can email and Skype."

Ella squeezed his fingers, her expression fierce. "We can make this work if that's what we both want."

Dillon connected with her gaze and held it. "It's what I want."

Ella gave a crisp nod. "I'm due at work this afternoon, but can I come home with you today? Spend time with you until Wednesday?"

"Yes." The gloom surrounding him lifted at her easy acquiescence. He stomped on the tiny part of him declaring this was too good to be true. He'd mess up somehow and lose the one woman he wanted. Instead of admitting any of his doubts, he smiled and kept smiling until the happy sentiment fit his mouth and stayed in place. "There is nothing I'd like better."

· ♥ · ♥ · ♥ · ♥ · ♥ ·

ELLA TWINED HER LEGS with Dillon's and savored the warmth of his big body. Despite the approach of spring, it was chilly this morning. She pressed a kiss against his chest and dragged in his musky scent.

"You're awake."

"Yes." She nipped his pectoral muscle hard enough to make him jump.

"The alarm will go off soon."

In reply, Ella sighed. She'd been trying not to imagine Dillon's departure and the danger he faced. Summer had taken her aside and told her not to be a stranger. She'd told—no, ordered Ella to ring or text or email her if she needed to unload. According to Summer, Dillon and her other brother Josh were skilled at their jobs, but Summer had an inkling of the emotions she'd experience with Dillon facing danger half a world away.

"I'll miss you." The truth as far as she was willing to admit.

Dillon broke their embrace and leaned over to switch on the bedside lamp. She blinked at the burst of light and drank in the tousled picture of sexiness. The hard muscles. His blue eyes and the black stubble shading his jaw. During their lovemaking, she'd noticed the old scars, although they hadn't discussed them.

"I've always been eager to join my team again," Dillon said, his gaze searching hers. "Not this time."

"Because of me?"

"You snuck up on me," Dillon said ruefully. "Hana helped me understand I'd lose you if I didn't admit to my...ah...affection for you."

Ella wrinkled her nose. "Should I apologize for crashing into your life?"

"Never." He opened his mouth to say more, but his phone buzzed. He slid out of bed and stopped the alarm.

"Are you sure you don't want to drive with us to the airport?"

"I've had so much time off work, and I'd hate to embarrass you by blubbering in public."

"You blubber? Surely not. Not the spitfire who barged into my life and told me off. Okay, before we go, I want to snap pictures of you and one of us together. Josh and my other friends will assume I'm spinning stories without photographic evidence. Bet he'll want to barge in on our Skype sessions." He grinned as he said this, affection for his sibling in his expression. "I'd better shower and get moving."

"I'll make coffee."

With a brief nod, Dillon strode from the bedroom and Ella unashamedly stared at his bare backside, taking visual pictures. She'd bring them back out during the night when she was missing him. As she filled the kettle with water and measured the coffee beans, she admitted to herself this separation might be harder than she'd assumed. Knowing Dillon was in danger and might die... She shook away the thought the instant it formed. No, she'd maintain her positivity and keep busy. She'd email Dillon all the local gossip and use this time apart as an opportunity to get acquainted.

Her phone rang, and she answered.

"Ella, it's Mike Hastings here. I'm sorry to ring you this early, but I'm heading out of town for two weeks. I've decided to sell the cottage. It goes on the market this morning. The real estate agent will be there just after nine to take photos."

"Oh?" Shock stole her ability to put sentences together.

Dillon's arm curled around her waist. "Something wrong?"

Could she buy the cottage herself? "How much are you asking for the cottage?"

"The agent said I should get five hundred thousand for it. Maybe more if I can attract the right buyer."

Ouch! Out of her price range. "How long do I have to move out?"

"You can stay until I get a buyer," Mike said. "I apologize for the short notice. You've been an excellent tenant, and if I wasn't desperate for the money, I'd be happy for you to stay. It's still possible the new purchaser will let you remain as a tenant."

Ella doubted that. She'd find somewhere else to stay, although it had taken a while to find her cottage. "It's all right, Mike. Thanks for telling me." She ended the call and turned to Dillon, her pulse racing with a burst of anxiety. "Mike Hastings needs money and he's selling my cottage."

"Easy," Dillon said without hesitation. "Move in here. As long as you don't mind the seclusion or walking Rufus. It should be safe enough now that the poachers are in jail."

"Are you sure? I enjoy it here, but..." She trailed off, not wanting to voice the fact their relationship was new and might not last this enforced separation.

"Dad is available if you need help. Connor will check on you. The main problem will be the blocked road. I doubt the council will bother clearing it in a hurry. Think about it, anyway."

Despite his obvious sincerity, she felt as if she was

taking advantage. No, that wasn't quite right. Although she liked Dillon, everything had happened between them so fast. For once, she was second-guessing her instincts and wondering if this time she might make a mistake. "Thanks, I will. The coffee is ready. I'll grab a quick shower. Ten minutes tops."

Ella hurried through her ablutions and left the house with Dillon. They didn't speak much during the drive to the landslide to meet Dillon's father, Ella dealing with weighty thoughts.

Dillon parked his vehicle and handed her the keys. "Move into my place, Ella. It would make me happy if you slept in my bed."

Ella studied his earnest expression. At the least, moving into Dillon's place would give her time to make plans for the future, but it still made her feel weird.

Dillon's father arrived just as they reached the other side of the blocked road.

"I will miss you." Dillon drew her against his chest and kissed her, heedless of their audience.

Ella clung, putting everything into their kiss. Her love. Fear. Her trepidation of what the future might bring. Her uneasiness at their separation.

"Son, I hate to end this farewell, but if we don't get moving, you'll miss your flight to Auckland."

Dillon pulled away from her, his callused fingertips stroking her cheek in a silent exchange that eased the worst of her anxiety. Then, he was gone, the vehicle disappearing around the bend and leaving an edgy silence and an uncertain future.

14

BACK IN AFGHANISTAN

"BRO!" JOSH, HIS YOUNGER brother, clasped him in a strong embrace before the rest of the men in his team greeted him one by one. Dillon scanned Josh and each of his brothers-in-arms and sensed something was off in that one quick glimpse. In the same instant, he realized he was done. He was ready to go home and stay with Ella.

"Something wrong? Where's Bull?"

"Our mission last night was fucked up from the start," Josh said. "The information we were sent from HQ was wrong, and we walked into the middle of an ambush. Bull went missing during the firefight."

"Missing," Dillon snapped out, fury digging into his features.

They didn't leave men. Never. Dead or alive, they brought them home.

"Who was running the mission?" Dillon asked. It

would've been him, had he been here.

"Guy from HQ," Josh muttered in disgust. "No field training in Afghanistan."

"Williams?"

Dillon turned to face a slim man in a crisp Army uniform. He bore an equally crisp English accent, which wasn't unusual since the NZSAS sometimes liaised with other countries. "Yes, sir." He had a strong sense he was facing the guy from HQ.

"My office once you've changed." The man swiveled and marched down the hall at a steady clip.

Dillon and the others eyed him until he disappeared.

"Guess I'd better get moving and discover what we're doing about our man," Dillon said. "Josh, I have things for you from home. Mum sent cookies."

"ANZAC biscuits?" Josh's voice held enthusiasm.

"Might be. Come and find out."

His brother followed him with an eagerness that reminded him of a puppy they'd had as kids. Jasper had lived to the ripe age of fifteen, and Dillon stilled missed the feisty Jack Russell.

"I met someone while I was at home," Dillon said.

"Mum might have spilled the beans. The parents are pleased, from what she said in her email. Do you have a picture?"

Dillon handed Josh his phone. His brother plugged in the password and thumbed to the photos. "The one with pink hair? Oh, yeah. Here's one of both of you. You look happy." Josh glanced at him, his blue eyes serious for once. "I'm glad you've found someone. After Hana, I worried about you. You changed."

"Guilt," Dillon confessed. "I wasn't there for Hana when she needed me. It's better now we've caught the men responsible. From what they said, Hana's death wasn't planned. She struck her head when she fell."

"Bro, cut the guilt shit. Hana was happy during her time in Eketahuna. She wrote to me. Mum and Dad loved her, and she made friends. You shouldn't worry or accept responsibility."

"Easy for you to say." Dillon wasn't about to admit Hana—the ghost Hana—had told him the same thing. "Josh, do me a favor?"

"Anything," his brother replied.

"If something happens contact Ella for me. Don't sugarcoat the truth. She's a strong woman, and if she has to worry, I'd prefer she received the facts. After Hana, I don't want secrets. Hana and I... I want to do things differently with Ella. Will you do that for me?"

"Nothing will happen to you." Josh radiated confidence. "But I will talk to Ella. I promise."

"Thanks." Dillon scowled as he buttoned his uniform shirt. "Better see what the boss wants."

The English man from HQ was a moron. Didn't take Dillon long to come to that decision.

"My gut is screaming about this mission," Josh muttered as they slipped through the darkness of an Afghani night.

The moon—a slim sickle in the sky above—gave off scant light but the night-vision goggles aided their eyesight. Acute silence. Nothing except his own breathing. His hackles raised. On instinct, he slowed and raised his hand in a signal for his group of five to do the same.

"It's too quiet." Hummer, a short, wiry man from north of Auckland, voiced all their concerns. The man had a gift with engines and delighted in taking them apart, especially Hummers, hence his nickname. "Something is off."

Dillon ran through the orders they'd been given and visualized the map in his head. "What if we backtrack and approach the village from the high ground?"

"Boss said it would take too long," Josh reminded him.

"Rather take too much time than walk into another trap," Frog declared. The man had a bulky, muscular body but moved with the grace of a panther. His nickname came not from his build but from his love of karaoke. The man couldn't sing to save himself.

"I agree. Let's retreat and approach from the high ground," Dillon said.

"Boss will have our arses," Hummer said.

Mitch and Kahu, the remaining members of their six-man team, nodded in agreement.

"My arse," Dillon stated. "Let's move out." His back itched as if someone was watching him. A thorough scan of the rocks, dust, and sand in their vicinity did nothing to reassure him. Still, the hair at the back of his neck prickled. Despite the night air, sweat coated his back and chest, making his shirt cling to his skin.

The rumble of voices had him freezing in position. His hand signal warned his men to still at his back, but they'd already caught the traveling sounds of chatter and slowed.

The ground in front of them rose at a steady incline, and about fifty feet ahead lay the crest of the hill. Dillon signaled for his men to wait and crept stealthily forward. He dropped onto his belly to crawl the last few feet.

A flock of sheep stood in a roughly constructed pen. Two young boys huddled around an open fire and the scent of roasting rabbit floated in his direction.

Reassured by the normalcy, he retraced his steps to join his waiting men. "Two young boys with their sheep," he murmured. "We'll retreat and circle these kids. We don't need them raising the alarm."

Silent nods were the only reply his men offered, and Dillon focused on the surrounding terrain, attempting to decide on the swiftest route to meet their objective—capturing or destroying the splinter group of militants who were causing problems for the locals and the military in the area. They'd need to follow the line of the cliff until it flattened out enough for them to scale the incline and trek to the coordinates given to them by HQ.

He signaled, and he and his men returned to the base of the rise. Dillon started along the bottom of the cliff, following a narrow path made by animals.

Josh tapped his shoulder. Dillon's pulse jumped—a shot of adrenaline flashing through his muscles—yet training held him still.

His brother leaned closer to whisper in his ear. "I got something. Movement at three o'clock. Must be a cave system."

Dillon focused on the area, and he spotted the shifting of a guard, bored with his post and moving to keep awake.

Bad mistake on his part.

He gestured for the men to press against the cliff to their right. Given the angle, the guard wouldn't spy their stealthy advance.

"The information from HQ was wrong. Again." Josh spoke in a hard voice, bitterness a slight layer beneath.

"Are we certain this isn't another group of innocent locals?" Frog asked.

"Only one way to find out," Dillon said. "Wait here." He took two steps when an anguished cry rippled from the direction of the guard.

"Bull," Josh whispered.

"Hold," Dillon ordered as each of the men instinctively surged forward. "We need to be clever about this. How many men were with the group that attacked you? A rough headcount."

"Ten," Josh replied. "Two died and the others got away. I'm certain we injured at least two."

"We'll go under the assumption they might have left one or two behind to guard their den. That means we should plan for at least ten to fifteen men. This group works with small mobile units, so with the element of surprise, we should grab the upper hand. Suggestions?"

"The guard looks bored," Frog said. "We need to take him out before they replace him with someone more alert."

"Agreed," Dillon murmured.

Another pained scream emerged from the cave, attracting the guard's attention.

"They're busy torturing Bull," Josh said in an urgent

voice. "Their attention is divided. Let Frog take out the guard and we'll move."

"Yeah, my thoughts exactly." Dillon nodded at Frog, and they watched their comrade melt into the darkness.

Dillon spared a brief thought for Ella and moved to Hana then smiled. Between the two, they'd make his life miserable if he didn't return home alive. Neither of them had spied Hana since the day of the lecture. Hopefully, she rested at peace now. He emptied his mind to focus on the mission and the enemy. Bull's broken cries bolstered his determination and the can-do will-do attitude from his men swirled around him. On this, they were of one mind. The SAS did not leave men behind.

Frog approached the sentry and pounced. The man crumpled without a sound, and Dillon and the others approached the cave. Didn't look as if any others were outside. Another jagged scream emerged from the confined space, but still none of the enemy exited the cave. No doubt the torture doubled as entertainment. These men were confident, which would be their downfall.

Dillon made a mental note to check where HQ had received their intel. Someone was feeding them a line, and that needed to stop.

He crept closer, weapon in hand, and cautiously rounded the lip of the cave. He hugged the wall while he took stock of what they faced. Eight men. A walk in the park. He glanced back and signaled the body count to his men and gestured them forward before focusing on the men with Bull. They'd be the first to die.

He waited a beat for his men to get in position.

Without warning, a shower of small rocks rained from the ceiling of the cave entrance. Dillon never hesitated. He fired two shots in rapid succession. The two men torturing Bull fell and didn't move again.

Now that they'd lost the element of surprise, his men came in hard and fast, diving low or hugging the wall. One of the enemies was clear-headed enough to grab a gun and return fire.

A bullet flicked fragments of rock from the cave wall. One dug into Dillon's cheek. He never stilled but fired, winging the third man.

Men shouted. The bang and whistle of ammunition filled the chamber with smoke and the acrid scent of hot weapons. A bullet hit Dillon in the chest, the oomph of power stealing his breath despite the protection of his vest. A second shot, a split second later punched through his shoulder. His vision narrowed to a pin prick as he fired a return shot. He felt himself crumpling, felt the thump as he met the ground and everything went black.

15

A CALL IN THE NIGHT

THE BIG BEN CHIME of Ella's phone woke her. She bolted upright, her heart pounding and a burst of fear blanking her mind. It was dark. Early. Chilly. Disoriented and groggy, she fumbled for the lamp switch. Her phone did a tiny dance showing a text, and she snatched it up.

Hey, Ella. It's Josh, Dillon's brother. I've sent you an email.

Another burst of anxiety had her fumbling with her phone. It took two attempts to get her email to pull through.

She scanned the subjects until she came to one from Dillon. She opened it.

Ella,

Josh here. Dillon zigged when he should've zagged and took a bullet to the shoulder. Our medic tended him almost straightaway and assures me Dillon will be fine although he hasn't regained consciousness yet. We got him back to base, and they've sent him to the hospital here for treatment. BTW, I don't know what you and Mum have been feeding him but he needs to go on a diet.

Dillon made me promise to contact you if something happened, but we'd both prefer if you didn't tell Mum and Dad yet. HQ will contact them this morning, anyway. I'll email or text you again once Dillon is out of surgery, and I have news.

You've done good with my big brother. He worried me for a while there. Can't wait to meet you in person.

Josh.

Ella read the email again, and despite Josh's upbeat manner, concern pressed against her chest, making her concentrate on each breath. Dillon had barely returned to Afghanistan and he was in surgery with at least one bullet hole in him. And he was still unconscious. That wasn't good.

Ella doubted she'd be able to sleep now. She checked the time on her phone. Five-thirty. She might as well rise. How long did an operation take? Ella pulled on a robe and thrust her feet into a pair of slippers.

She slipped her phone in her pocket and put the kettle on to make tea. Josh didn't email or text again, so she dressed and went out to take care of the alpacas and to let Rufus off for a run.

Just before nine, she walked into work with fear nipping at her heels. She wished she could talk to someone. Suzie was in Auckland—or was it Sydney? Since her friend had snagged a promotion, Ella had problems keeping her schedule straight. An email wasn't the same anyway because she desperately needed a hug.

This was a mistake. She should've stuck with casual. Friends with benefits. Then when Dillon had left, she could've moved on with happy memories. She should've... Heck! Her parents had taught her better than this. The pure selfishness of her thoughts had her uttering a small curse. Dillon was injured and lying in a hospital bed somewhere in Afghanistan, and he deserved her loyalty right now since she'd given him promises. Once he had recovered and he came home again—that would be her chance to reassess their relationship and lay out her fears.

With a nod to bolster this more positive plan, she settled into work for the day.

"I want you to lead the feeding of the eels tour this morning," her boss said.

"No problem," Ella said.

"We have a couple who have booked a private tour this afternoon." Marie handed over a sheet of paper. "This is their schedule. They particularly want to visit the kiwi house and the kaka feeding."

"Will do."

"If you can squeeze out time to restock the shop, I'd appreciate the help. The two coachloads of Japanese tourists yesterday decimated our stock. We have new T-shirts in as well. I'd like to get those loaded into our computer system."

Ella nodded, glad of the busy start to her day. Instead of

turning off her phone as was her normal habit at work, she switched it to vibrate and slipped it into her jeans pocket.

By the time the end of her workday arrived, the phone felt like a ticking bomb. Josh hadn't contacted her again. Neither of Dillon's parents had rung her with the news.

She wasn't sure what to do next.

·♥ · ♥ · ♥ · ♥ ·♥·

DILLON WOKE SLOWLY, THROBBING pain in his head. It vibrated down his neck to settle in his left shoulder. He didn't open his eyes but used his senses and foggy brain to ascertain his whereabouts.

A machine *beep-beep-beeped* to his left. Farther away, feminine voices murmured in English. American accents. Australian accents. And that *eh* at the end of a sentence sounded Canadian.

Safe.

He opened his eyes and turned his head. The throb of the tiny movement warned him to stop, but he required information. A groan forced its way up his throat. The croak halted the voices and sneakered feet tapped their way toward him.

"You're awake at last, Mr. Williams." A nurse with an Australian accent and strawberry blonde hair smiled at him. "We were starting to worry about you."

"Where am I?"

"At the military hospital. Still in Afghanistan." The nurse scrutinized his chart and made a notation.

"Ella," Dillon croaked, his throat and mouth

uncomfortably dry.

"Who is Ella?" She took his temperature and glanced at a monitor before she added something else to his chart.

"My girl. Phone." His head thumped without mercy, and he found it difficult to string together thoughts let alone words.

"Dillon, you're awake."

Dillon turned his head again to view the new arrival. A groan emerged and Josh hurried to his side.

"He's just woken. I need to call the doctor but you can have a few minutes with him before she arrives," the nurse said.

Josh dragged a chair closer to his bed and sat. "I brought your phone. How is the shoulder?"

"Throbbing like an alpaca kicked me. Head hurts worse."

Josh barked out a laugh. "We had to dive for cover when we retrieved you. Frog tripped and you bashed your head on a rock. The good news is we got Bull."

"He okay?"

"They say he will be," Josh said.

"Ella?"

"I emailed her, but that idiotic replacement from HQ has had us out backing the local guys. We've been out of range. I'll Skype her now and hold the phone for you."

"What time is it?"

"Middle of the night in New Zealand, but call her, anyway. She'll be worried."

"Mum and Dad?"

"I presumed HQ would contact them, but they haven't

called me demanding details," Josh said as he dialed the number.

It rang three times before Ella answered.

"Yes." Tension filled her voice.

"Ella, it's Josh. I'm in the hospital with Dillon. He wants to talk to you." Josh repositioned the phone and Ella's pale, anxious face came into view.

"Ella," he croaked. His head pounded, and the backs of his eyes stung, emotion a tangle in his chest. He loved this courageous woman. "Hi."

"You're okay," she whispered with a whoosh of relief. "I've been crazy worried. Once I realized your parents hadn't heard anything, I had no idea what to do. Josh didn't call, and I..." She swallowed hard.

"Crap, the doctor is here. Let me take the phone and I'll fill in the details for Ella," Josh said. "You can call her back once the doctor finishes poking and prodding."

"Thanks," Dillon said. The break would give him a chance to regain his equilibrium. Now wasn't the time to blurt out his love. He didn't know about Josh but his current contract was almost done. With his injuries, he doubted he'd be back, and this time he wouldn't be volunteering for another tour.

Dillon endured the examination and answered questions. "How bad is it, Doc?"

"The shoulder should heal well and you'll regain most of your function with physiotherapy. I was more concerned with your head injury. How's the pain level on a scale of one to ten?"

He went with honesty. "About a seven or eight."

"The nurse will get you painkillers and I'll schedule more tests. Any gaps in your memory?"

"The actual injury is hazy, but I remember being with my men and our mission goal."

The doctor stared at him as if she doubted his truthfulness but finally inclined her head. "If the pain worsens, inform the nurse."

"I will. How long will I be here?"

"I'll have more info once I get the test results, but at least a week. We're sending some of our patients home. As long as you improve and your headaches reduce, you'll make that plane to New Zealand."

"Thanks, Doc."

With another nod, the doctor strode from his room. Josh's laughter floated from the corridor outside and came closer after the doctor left.

"Do you want me to hold the phone for you?"

"Please," Dillon said.

"Ella said no one contacted Mum and Dad. She panicked a bit when I went radio-silent," Josh said.

"I stressed enough for your entire family," Ella admitted. "But I figured if the Army hadn't contacted them you must be alive."

"The doctor told me as long as my headaches resolve and the tests come back okay, they should ship me home in a week," Dillon said.

"That's great," Ella said, her eyes lighting and color creeping into her cheeks. "Rufus misses you."

"Only Rufus?"

"I miss you," Ella said. "Is Josh still there?"

"He's holding the phone. Go back to bed, sweetheart. I'll ring you again at a more reasonable time. Hopefully, I'll have an update then."

"What about your parents?"

"I'll ring them," Josh said.

"Bye." Dillon ached to hold her, the yearning filling him with resolve. Hana had been right. He and Ella were perfect for each other. While she'd verbally committed to him and the sex was great, it was time to court her and learn more about her likes and dislikes. Her passions. From now on, he intended to do everything in his power to convince Ella they had a future together.

"You like her," Josh said once Dillon ended the call.

"Ella is going to be your new sister-in-law."

Josh's brows shot upward, his mouth dropping open in surprise. "You haven't known each other for long."

"Hana liked her."

"But Ella said she hasn't lived in Eketahuna for long. Hana died before she arrived."

Dillon grinned, despite the ache in his head. Revealing this story to his practical brother who bore the same black-and-white view of the world that Dillon had shared before Ella—was gonna be fun.

· ❤ · ❤ · ❤ · ❤ · ❤ ·

THREE WEEKS LATER, ELLA arrived home from work to find Rufus running free. The dog let out an excited bark of greeting and raced to meet her. Ella halted. The front door was wide open. Panic ripped through her until she realized a thief wouldn't wedge a stop beneath the wooden door to keep it open. Dillon appeared and joy rippled through her. She ran and skidded to a stop in front of him, a grin on her face.

"You're home."

They'd talked most days, and she'd learned he liked casual clothes, reading mysteries and humor. He enjoyed rock music, and green was his favorite color. One day he wanted to visit Greece because mythology interested him.

"For good," he said with clear satisfaction.

"I... Can I hug you?" He'd told her he intended to resign, although he wasn't sure what he'd do as a job.

"The doctor gave me the all-clear yesterday."

She gripped his shoulders and pressed close. His citrus scent filled her with satisfaction while his hard strength sent her thoughts in another direction. "No more headaches?"

"Not a one. I need to keep going with the exercises the physio gave me for my arm, but other than that, they're pleased with my progress."

Ella scanned his face and the dark scruff on his jaw that gave him a dangerous air, especially when combined with the intensity of his blue gaze. Her nipples pulled tight and her stomach did a slow flip. "Can we have sex? Right now?"

He closed one eye in a wink. "I thought you'd never ask."

"Oh no." Ella backed away, her hands raised in protest as he offered a devilish smile. "You're not carrying me to the bedroom."

"Move faster then."

Ella chortled. Once she'd skipped past him, she slowed to a hip-rolling amble. A groan came from behind her, and her grin widened.

"I missed you."

In the bedroom, Ella turned to face him and waited for him to comment on the changes she'd made. A picture on the wall. A vase of flowers she'd picked in the garden. Two extra pillows. A mohair throw rug.

"The house is more alive than it was when I was on my own here."

"You don't mind if I make changes?"

"I enjoy the new ambiance —your possessions mingled with mine. Now, where were we?"

Her lips curved, and she sashayed toward the bed. With her gaze on Dillon, she tugged her uniform polo shirt over her head then unbuttoned her jeans and eased them down her legs.

"Sexy black underwear. Have I told you I like lace?"

"A happy coincidence. I didn't have time to do the laundry." She cocked her head. "Perhaps I should do it now."

"No way! Help me with my T-shirt?"

Ella closed the distance between them. She slid her hands over his chest and lifted the hem of his navy-blue T-shirt. The ridges of his abdomen, the splendid array of muscles was the same, but the puckered redness of the wound on his left shoulder proved how close she'd come to losing him.

"Don't."

Ella didn't pretend confusion. "Your shoulder…"

"You can't worry about what might have happened. I'm here, alive and ready to celebrate the fact."

With deft hands, she unfastened his faded jeans and tugged them and his boxer-briefs down his legs. She scanned him and licked her lips. "Lay on the bed. I'm happy to do the work this time."

He followed her suggestion with alacrity, his eyes aglow, his head bobbing. "You're killing me, woman. I've been imagining this moment since I left Afghanistan. Hell, before that."

"I've missed you. Not just the sex but sleeping beside you and waking in your arms." Her gaze drank him in as he stretched out on the big bed. "I can't decide where to feast first."

"Come closer. I can give you hints."

Amusement bubbled in her, tickling like champagne and making her realize she hadn't laughed as much recently. She'd worried about Dillon since Josh had let slip he was still getting headaches. "Not necessary. So many spots to taste and nibble. So little time."

"Today, please."

Ella grinned, her mood lighthearted. "I've decided to start here."

She tugged on his big toe and ran her fingertips over the sole of his foot. He jerked it away.

"Ah. Something to remember."

He bared his teeth in a growl.

"All right. Moving along." Ella urged him to part his thighs. "One day I'd like to sketch you like this."

"You draw?"

"Badly," she admitted. "But I'd happily perfect my basic skills with you as my model." She skimmed a gentle finger along the length of his erection and circled the bulbous head. A drop of pre-come beaded at the tip and she rubbed it into his skin.

"Ella, I won't last long this first time."

She nodded and sat back, one hand creeping between her legs to soothe her aching flesh. "The honest truth. I used my vibrator last night after our phone call because I was missing you, but it wasn't the same." She hummed, enjoying the easy glide of her finger over her clit.

Dillon cleared his throat.

"Oh, are you waiting?"

"Minx. You wait until I'm one hundred percent fit. Your backside will be a pretty blushing pink."

"Promises. Promises." Humming, Ella reached for the bedside drawer and pulled out a strip of condoms. She ripped one open and rolled it efficiently on Dillon's shaft.

"You're pretty. Perhaps I should sketch too. I'd happily draw you. Your perky breasts. Your pink and purple hair. Did I tell you I like the addition of the purple?"

"No, you told me last night you thought you'd like it."

"I was right."

"Wow, that there is masculine smugness." She pulled a face at him.

"Come closer. I want to kiss you."

"Soon." Ella positioned herself and filled her channel with his cock. A unified groan filled the bedroom. With an evil grin, she squeezed her internal muscles, her flesh clutching and releasing rhythmically.

When Dillon cursed, she rose and sank back down, savoring the fullness of his erection.

"Please, Ella. I need a kiss. I've waited so long."

Ella swayed toward him and fitted her lips to his. Their mouths lingered and clung in an intoxicating meeting before hunger took over. Dillon's hand slipped behind her neck and held her in place. His lips devastated her. The long-drugging kiss blanked everything else from her mind, and when their mouths finally parted, she smiled. "Wow."

Dillon stared back at her, a softness in his expression that wasn't normally present. His steady regard flustered her. She opened her mouth and closed it again. Heat filled her cheeks. Had she scared him? She didn't think so, but men's minds were a mystery to her.

"Are you stopping?"

"What? No." Ella rocked her hips forward, lifting, falling and straining to achieve the perfect angle.

"Faster," Dillon ordered in a harsh voice. "Touch yourself again."

She obeyed, her finger skidding across her slippery clit. She jumped when he flicked a nipple and focused on him.

"Good." He added a pinch to her nipple and the hint of pain shoved her straight into climax. It roared through her, leaving her breathless and trembling.

Dillon stroked upward, his hard cock prolonging the pulses in her pussy. Then he gripped her hips, his harsh groan echoing throughout the bedroom, his expression strained as he found his release. Gradually, his grip on her hips lessened and he opened his blue eyes.

"I love you, Ella. Will you marry me?"

"But we've barely spent a week together."

"I'm a decisive man. I'm confident in my decision. Come here."

She parted their bodies and removed the condom for Dillon before reclining on the bed beside him. He wrapped his arms around her.

"It's true our short acquaintance has been drama-filled, but I do understand you. You love color. All colors. You have a huge collection of sexy vintage dresses, and you can't wait for the warmer weather so you can wear them instead of your jeans. You prefer comfortable underwear but you have a few sexy pairs for special occasions. For reading, you prefer romance and mysteries. Your favorite author is Ilona Andrews because you like sexy heroes and kickass heroines. Should I go on?"

"You listened to me."

"I wasn't asking questions to fill out the conversation. You fascinate me. You have from the start."

"Really? You hated it when I barged into your life to inform you of my resident ghost."

"But I came to appreciate your tenacity, your courage, and your sassy attitude. Ella, you're everything I need in a woman. Hana was right about us being perfect together. I love you. I'm certain about that."

All the fight, the lingering shock melted away. "Aw, Dillon." She rolled over and kissed him, allowing her emotions to surface. When she parted their mouths, she caressed his cheek. "Are you home for good?"

"Yes. I'm a patient man. I can wait for you to sort out your head."

Ella snapped her fingers in front of his face. "No, Dillon Williams. I do love you. When we're apart, you're all I can think of, and I lived for your phone calls and the chats. It's the marriage part that makes me hesitate."

"That can be a long-term strategy." Dillon's gaze connected with hers. "Live with me and love me. The rest will fall into place. What do you say?"

Hana had been convinced she and Dillon were perfect for each other. "Yes."

"Yes?"

"I like the idea of walking into the future with you."

"My parents adore you. Josh is halfway in love with you. Summer told me I should move fast before someone else grabbed you first. Hana has given her seal of approval, and I'm crazy about you."

Happy tears filled Ella's eyes. "Yes."

With a broad grin, Dillon kissed her, and they didn't leave the bedroom for a long, long time.

EPILOGUE

THE WEDDING, FIVE MONTHS LATER

"IT'S TIME." SUMMER SMILED in approval. "You look beautiful. Are you certain you want to marry my brother?"

"I like him a lot." Was crazy in love with him, actually.

A knock came on the bedroom door. "Summer, are you and Ella ready? Your mother sent me to tell you everyone is waiting," Nikolai called through the door.

"We're ready. We'll be there in a few minutes," Summer said. "Well, if you're sure you want my bossy brother."

"Positive." Ella picked up her casual bouquet of white flowers and greenery and straightened the pale slate-blue skirt of her gown. Her hair held fresh highlights in three shades of pink and she wore it in a messy updo.

Summer grabbed her bouquet and scanned her appearance in the full-length mirror. She wore a slender gown in a darker shade of blue. She opened the door and held it for Ella. "Let's do this."

Ella followed Summer out to the garden where Dillon's family and their friends waited. One of their friends played his guitar.

Suzie darted around with her camera, snapping shots of her and Summer while Dillon waited with Josh and the wedding celebrant beneath an arbor of trailing blue and white ribbons and white potted roses.

Ella's gaze drifted to Dillon who wore a shirt of a similar hue to her dress and black trousers. Their gazes connected, and a rush of emotion grabbed her. Since Dillon's return home, they'd grown even closer, and Ella had said yes to Dillon's proposal without hesitation.

When Ella reached Dillon's side, he took her right hand in his and kissed her cheek. "You look beautiful."

"Hey! Save that for later," Josh said, his loud voice making everyone laugh including Mrs. Geneva, the wedding celebrant.

"We are here today to witness the marriage of Dillon and Ella..." Mrs. Geneva moved through the vows. "I now pronounce you man and wife."

Dillon drew Ella close and kissed her. Cheers and wolf-whistles filled the garden as the kiss continued.

"Ella. Dillon."

Ella jerked away from her new husband while Dillon stared in the direction the voice had come from.

"Do you see her?" Ella whispered.

"Yeah."

Hana waved at them with a broad grin. "Name your first girl after me."

"That's a promise," Dillon murmured.

"You'll have a strong, happy marriage," Hana promised. "I have to leave. Goodbye."

As they watched, Hana faded from sight. Dillon kissed Ella again, and they turned to face their families and friends.

"None of them saw Hana," Ella said

"No, but it's good to have her blessing."

"It is."

And together Ella and Dillon stepped forward to celebrate their marriage and the beginning of their life together.

·♥·♥·♥·♥·♥·

THANK YOU FOR READING *Stranded with Ella.* How did you enjoy Ella and Dillon's adventures with the ghost? I'd love to hear your thoughts, so please consider leaving a review at your favorite online bookstore, Goodreads, or Bookbub. A review would make my day!

Josh's story is next. He does a favor for a friend and meets a woman who might just be perfect for him. Learn more about Josh's Fake Fiancee. (www.shelleymunro.com/books/joshs-fake-fiancee)

If you'd like to keep up with my releases, check out my newsletter (www.shelleymunro.com/newsletter/)

About Author

USA Today bestselling author Shelley Munro lives in Auckland, the City of Sails, with her husband and a cheeky Jack Russell/mystery breed dog.

Typical New Zealanders, Shelley and her husband left home for their big OE soon after they married (translation of New Zealand speak - big overseas experience). A twelve-month-long adventure lengthened to six years of roaming the world. Enduring memories include being almost sat on by a mountain gorilla in Rwanda, lazing on white sandy beaches in India, whale watching in Alaska, searching for leprechauns in Ireland, and dealing with ghosts in an English pub.

While travel is still a big attraction, these days Shelley is most likely found in front of her computer following another love - that of writing stories of contemporary and paranormal romance and adventure. Other interests include watching rugby (strictly for research purposes), cycling, playing croquet and the ukelele, and curling up with an enjoyable book.

Visit Shelley at her Website
www.shelleymunro.com

Join Shelley's Newsletter
www.shelleymunro.com/newsletter

ALSO BY SHELLEY

Military Men
Innocent Next Door
Soldier with Benefits
Safeguarding Sorrel
Stranded with Ella
Josh's Fake Fiancee
Operation Flower Petal
Protecting the Bride

Friendship Chronicles
Secret Lovers
Reunited Lovers
Clandestine Lovers
Part-Time Lovers
Enemy Lovers
Maverick Lovers
Sports Lovers

SHELLEY MUNRO

Fancy Free
Protection
Romp
Buzz
Festive

Single Titles
One Night of Misbehavior
Playing to Win
Reformed Bad Girl

Milton Keynes UK
Ingram Content Group UK Ltd.
UKHW012308060524
442290UK00004B/219

9 781991 063489